# Praise
# In *Julia's* Garden

When a stranger leaves an old journal in her office, landscape architect Lily McGuire will need all her gardening expertise to unravel its secrets. Does the disappearance of the journal's author, 1940s socialite Julia, have any connection to the recent death of Lily's boss? And will Lily allow herself to consider a relationship with attractive co-worker, Jack Chapman? *Julia's Garden* is an intriguing puzzle mystery with a determined heroine searching not only to find Julia but also to find a new pathway for her own life.

**— Jane Tesh Author of the *Madeline Maclin Mysteries* and *The Grace Street Series***

Intelligent but alone, and burying her once adventurous spirit in her work, landscape architect Lily McGuire is lured by an odd stranger to solve an age-old mystery he believes is planted somewhere within the pages of an old gardening journal. An irritatingly intrepid and handsome colleague pulls Lily off-course in her resolve to sulk in the fetid remains of her years-old failed marriage, while assisting her in digging around in the potentially deadly mystery, dating back to the 1940s. Laura S. Wharton's Lily must dig deep to reconstruct not only the mystery *In Julia's Garden*, but to redesign her own outlook on life in the process.

**— Mary Flinn Award-winning author of**
***The One, Second Time's a Charm, Three Gifts, A Forever Man, The Nest* and *Breaking Out***

# In *Julia's* Garden

## A LILY McGUIRE MYSTERY

Laura S. Wharton

***In Julia's Garden***
*A Lily McGuire Mystery*


Address all inquiries to:
Broad Creek Press
253 Farmbrook Road
Mt. Airy, NC 27030

Wharton, Laura S.
In Julia's Garden/by Laura S. Wharton
Mt. Airy, NC: Broad Creek Press, 2015
813.54
p. cm – (In Julia's Garden)

Summary: Landscape architect Lily McGuire is lured by an odd stranger to solve a potentially deadly mystery dating back to the 1940s when he presents her with an old gardening journal.

Library of Congress Control Number: 2015913704
Print Book ISBN: 978-0-9904662-9-1

[1. Mystery—Fiction. 2. Adventure—Fiction. 3. North Carolina—Fiction. 4. Gardening—Fiction.]

Printed in the United States of America

# Dedication

For Kathy.

—LSW

# Other Novels By
# Laura S. Wharton

**Award-winning novels for Young Adults and Adults:**

*Stung! A Sam McClellan Tale*
*Deceived: A Sam McClellan Tale*
*Leaving Lukens*
*The Pirate's Bastard*

**Award-winning mysteries for Children:**

*Mystery at the Lake House #1: Monsters Below*
*Mystery at the Lake House #2: The Mermaid's Tale*
*Mystery at the Lake House #3: The Secret of the Compass*
*Mystery at the Phoenix Festival*
*The Wizard's Quest*

All titles are available as print and e-books.
To learn more about Laura's other books,
visit www.LauraWhartonBooks.com

# Chapter One

"Are you the one they call 'Lily McGuire'?" The man's frame nearly filled the doorway of my office. Solid as a statue, he waited for me to look up from my cluttered desk.

"I am," I sighed, aggravated at yet another interruption. This day was turning out to be highly unproductive. Lowering my tortoise-shell reading glasses past the bridge of my nose, I marked my place in the dusty book lying open on my desk and looked up. A slightly audible gasp slipped from my lips as I took in the sight in front of me. This man didn't look like the bureaucrats I had been dealing with during the many planning meetings I'd had to attend in person, or sound like the ones who talked incessantly during weekly phone conferences. No, this man looked more like someone to avoid making eye contact with in the park on an early morning jog. His shaggy silver hair and unkempt beard skewed in every direction. A ragged brown coat hung loosely on his frame, which I guessed to be well over six feet tall—and no hunched shoulders, either. Guessing his age, I pegged him to be about ninety, though who could tell under all that hair? Regaining my composure, I rose and extended my hand. Mud-caked boots stood rooted, even as I motioned for him to enter my small office, which was tidy except for my desk. "You have me at a disadvantage, Mister…?"

"Evans. You can call me Evans." Still not moving from his spot, Mr. Evans pulled a small package from under the enormous coat. "I have something for you. It's from…her. It may help." Hesitating, Mr. Evans carefully fingered the box, neatly wrapped in brown craft paper. His fingers toyed slowly, seemingly absent-mindedly, with the pale blue ribbon encircling the package. He looked at it, then at me, as if gauging my trustworthiness.

Wondering whether Mr. Evans could sense my discomfort, I got up from my chair and moved around the desk to stand in front of him. Slowly, I held out my hand in an attempt to accept the package. Being so close to him, I smelled a strong odor of decaying plant matter on him—not just from his boots—it was emanating from his person. Above the smell of dirt, though, were the most brilliant blue eyes I think I've ever seen. They were almond-shaped and crinkled around the edges. He was smiling, like he knew a dirty little secret.

"Interesting thing about this package, you know," he began, holding the small box firmly while stroking its encircling ribbon tenderly with his other hand. "It contains *all* the secrets of Julia's garden. She told me so herself, she did." Mr. Evans never looked away from my eyes, though his hands continued to fondle the package. "I often watched her as she wrote things in it. Names of plants, sure, you'll find those. Dates of their plantings… you'll find that, too. There's more, though. Much more. You may have to read it more than once to find what you're looking for. I read it so many times, I could quote passages for you. The one item I never found mentioned in it was something I want to find—have to find. Perhaps you will." With these words, Mr. Evans relinquished his treasure to me. No more hesitation, no flourish.

With some of its mystery diluted, I accepted Mr. Evans' package and smiled a well-practiced (though not entirely genuine) smile. He had brought his treasure from South Carolina, a three-hour drive at best. Fearing he might want to hang around while I looked it over, I quickly spoke. "Thank you for bringing it. I hope you didn't go to too much trouble to do so. You could have mailed it to me. If you'll leave an address with our receptionist or your business card with me, I will return it when I'm done reviewing it." I extended my hand, expecting to shake Mr. Evans' hand before he left. He didn't extend his hand. Nor did he budge.

I buffeted myself for what I thought would be the inevitable speech to come, one more opinion on how my job should be done. "Is there something else you'd like to share?"

The smile disappeared from Mr. Evans' face as he spoke. "Only this: many people have been hurt because of what's inside. Your boss lady died over it." He looked away. His eyes focused sharply once again on me. "Don't be the next." Mr. Evans turned and left my office like a man who had completed his mission. He left me with a vacuum of thoughts to sift through. And the package.

# Chapter Two

Alone again in the cool of my plant-filled office, I tossed the package on the credenza behind my desk and rubbed my eyes. *Great*, I thought. *One more artifact to sift through. It's going to be another long night.* Generally, not much fazed me. I'd seen my fair share of odd people sporting what they thought were *treasures* during various historic garden renovation projects: old maps and journals of accounts and plants, crumbling architectural drawings, most of which my visitors shared excitedly. Frequently, I had been accosted when I was on site visits in Columbia, South Carolina, by preservation-minded people voicing their opinions over what I should and should not do to preserve one of their city's most beloved (and, in my own not-so-humble opinion, decrepit) historic gardens and its adjoining manor house. Of course, as a landscape designer, my portion of the job ended where the walls of the great house began. Still, as was often pointed out to me (as if I didn't know), what I was doing had to be in concert with a house's preservation. My house of current interest was the Norton-Grace Mansion, one of the most enduring landmarks in Columbia. It harkened back to a more genteel antebellum era when people had time to meander through a garden of eight acres and marvel at its glories or enjoy being surrounded by fragrant flowers under a dappled canopy of tree cover.

The project was a state away from me and required a lot of site visits, Preservation Commission meetings, and time away from my own little garden. Yet the task of managing the renovation of this historic garden fell to me when Macy Lachaise, the founder of the landscape designing firm where I work, dropped dead of an apparent heart attack at the age of forty-two. That was one year ago. Macy was the project's lead designer and an advocate of garden restoration in the southeastern landscape design community. She was as vocal as she was vibrant. A diva and community mover and shaker, she was an original. A distant relative of the French-American sculptor Gaston Lachaise, Macy was the complete opposite of me. (I'd guess most people would say I'm reserved, or maybe even a tad misanthropic. I wouldn't agree with that summation, of course.) I was drawn to Macy, as were most professionals here in Winston-Salem, North Carolina, as well as in other Southern cities the firm served. Macy had the ability to make every person who knew her feel like he or she was her very *best* friend. She actually was mine.

What did this crusty Mr. Evans mean by saying the package he gave me caused Macy's death? The nerve of him, stirring up a hornet's nest of feelings about that, about her, after all this time. The attending physician,

Dr. Tesh, assured us it was a heart attack a year ago—probably too much stress from the job. She did her best to comfort Macy's family and those of us from the firm who were at the hospital that night, but I suspected her heart wasn't in it. Dr. Tesh knew Macy, too. Everyone did. Macy was a force of nature. It was a shame she was taken from us so soon. We mourned, all of us. The funeral service was full of friends and family. It seemed like the entire design community turned out for the event. When that was over, we worried about what to do with the business. We continued to carry on in her honor, in her memory. At first, it was hard for me to be at work every day, waiting for her raucous laughter to reverberate through the wall that divided her office from mine in this converted tobacco warehouse downtown. After a while, I numbed myself to her memory so I could focus on work.

I guess I had been doing fine, mostly, until this moment. Clients continued to extend their condolences to me…to all of us. Maybe they felt sorry for us, but they still accepted our proposals. One year had passed, and the firm was still open for business. I was doing better with it these days. Or at least I thought I was, until Mr. Evans brought up her death.

And he wanted me to believe it was because of that little package? No way. Perhaps Mr. Evans was being a bit melodramatic, making his offering seem more important than anything else on my cluttered desk today. Well, it wasn't going to work. I had a deadline to meet.

I plopped down in my favorite chair, a turquoise Ekornes opposite my desk, and twirled a strand of my already kinky brown hair. The cut I had thought I was getting didn't turn out anything like the picture in the magazine I had so cautiously shared with my hairstylist, someone I thought I could trust, given the string of disasters I had endured at the hands of other stylists. I was almost used to the cut this week. It would grow back. Full, thick, and bordering on riotous, my hair was as unruly as my desk appeared. I hated a cluttered desk, but it was a fast-approaching deadline that kept it in this state of confusion.

The deadline was for yet another grant I had to help the Norton-Grace Preservation Commission with on this project. A grant writer had been on staff for a year or so, but budgets got tight, so the commission had let her go and decided to do without. The commission had managed to write this grant without much help. Well, most of it. The last three requirements on the request for funds had to come from my office.

This was always Macy's bailiwick, the getting-money-out-of-anybody task. When Macy died, her marketing, schmoozing, and grant-writing duties were divided among the remaining partners and staff of the small design firm of Lachaise & Associates, P.A. The partners quickly agreed that schmoozing wasn't one of my strong suits, so filling out grant requirements became my task. So far, I had struck out on two of the last five grant requests I had attempted for this project.

The commission had raised a great deal of money on its own before we got the project, but a bit more was needed that wasn't available from the community of Columbia. Without the extra funding that the grants would provide, the commission could not afford to implement the full plan Macy and the rest of the team had so carefully laid out for the gardens. I felt responsible for the entire project, and it weighed heavily on me. Handling this kind of pressure was not my strong suit, either.

I extricated myself from my cozy chair and resumed the position at my desk. Try as I might, I couldn't focus on the matter at hand. I swiveled around to the credenza where the plain package wrapped in blue ribbon lay beside a moody black and white photo I had taken of my college-aged son, stoic looking as he manned a sailboat's wheel through choppy waves. It was one of my favorite pictures of Ben, though it was a reminder of his pending graduation and leap into a new adventure of which I would not be part. I straightened the picture, then picked up another one for the two of us dressed in our white karate gi outfits. Ben was ten, and had just earned his yellow belt. The smile on his face was huge, and I remembered that day so clearly. It was a turning point for both of us.

"Another plant journal," I moaned to nobody in particular. I picked it up, carefully untied the ribbon, and let it drift to the floor. Unable to forget Mr. Evans' admonition, I unwrapped the brown paper from the package as if it contained a pressure-sensitive bomb detonator. No such luck. I was almost disappointed: in my hands was a four-by-six-inch leather-bound journal with rough-edged, yellowed pages. Rhinestones of varying shades of red and purple surrounded neat lettering, claiming this was, indeed, the belonging of someone named Julia. I carefully opened the cover. The book's spine was a mush of string and crumbling glue. The leather on the cover had held up well for decades, but the pages were tattered in places, smudged in spots with dirt or something else. Flipping through the pages for a quick scan, I noticed it was less of a gardening journal and more of a diary with dated entries. I reached for my tortoise-shell reading glasses and turned the page.

*June 8, 1944*

*What a party! My sixteenth birthday celebration! Everyone was here. Well, nearly everyone I care about, truthfully. The Hodges came. Sissy looks positively scandalous in red, but she's always had that way about her. Timmy and Edith came in matching blue, hers chiffon and his a pale shirt that set his eyes glowing. They make the cutest couple. Gerald came with Rachel. I adore Rachel, but her taste in men leaves something to be desired. Oh, well, to each her own. Let's see, the Crosbys, Jenkins, Reiners, and Flinns all came. The Adams children were adorable, and they loved splashing in the fountain. Mary was there, of course, and she brought her new beau, Mike. Jane came, too, so I had all my friends with me for my special day. The gardens looked fabulous, as always. I can't imagine a more bountiful spring! Flowers blossomed everywhere, and I was so pleased to see that many of the varieties lasted despite the recent heat we've had.*

*And the music! Music was everywhere, thanks to Sid. I adore his little band of merry-makers. They did it up right, despite two of their people being absent. I noticed, of course, because Jimmy wasn't here. I know he said he'd be here for the party, but he didn't show up with the quartet. I hope he'll stop by later to redeem himself, but maybe he'll stop by tomorrow.*

*Betsey did a fine job with the food, as usual. I do admire her ability to pull magic out of thin air. Whenever I've snooped in her kitchen for a late-night snack, I'm dismayed at the emptiness of it all. I'm not sure we had all that food she prepared in the cupboard, but she's just brilliant when it comes to creating menus. I couldn't have asked for better.*

*Of course, my parents were there, too, looking as sharp as ever. I don't suppose others my age might get along as well with their parents as I do, but mine are exceptional. I guess I'm prejudiced, being as how they are mine, but truly, they've done so much with so little that to throw me this grand party is amazing. I'm grateful, yet I'm aware of what's going on around town. A reminder just flew overhead in the way of a training plane. The Columbia Army Base is quite the military airfield, with its pilots training bomber crews. A few of us stopped by last month and saw the 96th Air Base Squadron at work. Lee Bowman's band played there at a U.S.O. dance. What fun that was! There's going to be a Red Cross social next month, and there's talk of more G.I. dances. Mama says I'm too young to go, but as long as I go with the gang, I think she'll let me attend. Besides, it's our civic duty to entertain the troops.*

*My flashlight's battery is getting weak, so I'll close for now…oh, my…who is this wandering up the garden path? Could it be him? It's nearly too dark to see.*

The question mark ending the journal entry sent my eyebrows up. Seems the young Miss Julia was having a fine time of it. *Good for her,* I thought.

"Knock, knock." Jack Chapman was standing in the doorway, rapping on the doorjamb for added impact. "Anybody home?" His 1980s rock band concert T-shirt looked to me like it should have been retired when the one-hit wonder band stopped touring years ago. The rust color of his shirt matched the color of his baggy Carhartt pants, which looked pristine compared to his battered hiking boots.

Snapping out of my waltz through Julia's little garden party, I looked up when Jack took a step inside. "Oh, hi, Jack."

"Don't look so disappointed, Lil." He sounded a bit disappointed himself.

I chose to ignore the way he cut my name short. It had been a long day, and I truly didn't want to get into it over that…again. "Sorry, Jack; I was just going over some old journals and paperwork, trying to pull all the loose ends together on this grant. How are you?" I feigned excitement the best I could.

"Well, Lil, I'm just great," Jack sang out in his usual chipper way. "I'm about to head out the door. You do realize it's time to stop for the day, don't you?"

"I still have a bit of work to do here," I said flatly.

"And you have karate practice this evening that you can't miss. You agreed to help with the younger students. They are testing for belt ranks, remember?"

I groaned. "Thanks for the reminder. I had forgotten about that. Okay. I'll close up here in a few minutes. I have to run home to get my karate gi, but I'll see you at the dojo in a bit."

"I can swing by and pick you up if you like."

"What, and ride me on the handlebars of your bike? No thanks; I'll drive myself." I had to smile at the thought of the two of us riding through the Winston-Salem traffic that way. Jack did it all the time, but I wouldn't dare.

"Actually, I've got the Blazer running, and she needs to get out a bit."

"Then absolutely no thanks," I said emphatically. "I don't think that hunk of junk is ready for the roads yet—maybe it never, ever will be again. You should probably put it out of its misery and have it hauled to the nearest junkyard." I placed the journal carefully on the credenza, knowing I'd have to read it through tomorrow. "I still haven't figured out why you would want to keep it around all these years. What is it—thirty years old next year? No, thanks. I'll just see you at karate."

"I'm offended." Jack mocked me, holding his hands to his heart. "That Blazer is a classic. It ran just fine back when

I bought her used in college. She just needs a little fine-tuning, that's all. Then she'll outrun anything on the roads."

"As long as you have a spare tank of gas in the back, sure. What does it get? Two miles to the gallon?"

Looking chastised, Jack shuffled his feet and shrugged. "A bit more than that, if you really want to know. Besides, just think of all the plants she can haul." His voice sounded optimistic, as if this nudge would be the one that worked to get me to accept his offer of a ride. It didn't.

"I'm thinking that's a grand reason to keep an old vehicle, but I've come to the conclusion that I'll still drive myself to karate tonight." I waved him off, as if trying to shoo away an annoying fly from a picnic. I stood up and stretched my arms overhead. Then I surveyed the mess on my desk. Ugh. Tomorrow was going to be a long one.

"Have it your way, Lil. Toodle-oo." Jack smiled that brilliant smile of his and waved as he strolled out of my office and turned down the hall toward the main entrance lobby. I heard him call out his good nights to Stephanie Young, the receptionist, whom I happened to know had a crush on him. I suspected he got that a lot, though. He was a rugged kind of handsome and an extremely talented man who liked a good joke and a fast flirt. He absolutely did nothing for me, though, with dark hair hanging down in his boyish face. Definitely not my type. Not that I had any particular type in mind at the moment, but I knew Jack Chapman wasn't it.

I looked around at the mess in front of me, sighed, and did my best Scarlett O'Hara impersonation. "Tomorrow is another day," I muttered to nobody in particular. I hated the thought of leaving such clutter to greet me in the morning, but Jack was right. I did promise to help with the younger students' belt rank tests this evening. The thought of seeing their excited faces brought a smile to my own, sufficient enough to bolster me from feelings of dread for the next day's workload. I turned off my computer and desk lamp before closing the door that would hide my inability to leave a tidy office and hopefully discourage the cleaning crew from disturbing any of the papers on my desk.

"I'm heading out, Steph," I called to Stephanie as I approached the lobby. Knowing she didn't like to be left at the office alone, I dawdled for a few moments in the lobby as she pulled on her bright lime green raincoat.

We were typically the last two there most nights, so this was our routine: Stephanie cleaned up the coffeepot and tidied the kitchen precisely at four o'clock. (If anyone wanted coffee after that, she might acquiesce, but she'd be peeved at her routine being set out of whack.) Then she would turn off her computer at the receptionist desk precisely at five o'clock, taking care to sign the log book she kept of visitors and the one she kept for partners and associates. Stephanie was a stickler for details. She needed to know where everyone was all the time, and she made few exceptions for partners and associates who forgot to sign in or out through "her" lobby. I say few exceptions because I'd watched often enough as she'd fill in times for Jack Chapman, the darling of the firm, who was as negligent in this duty as he was brilliant with the civil engineering services he brought to each project. Yeah, Stephanie definitely had a crush on Jack.

Our last bit of ritual was to set the alarm and turn off the master switch for the lights, which were programmed for motion detection throughout the racetrack-like office. Then we'd head out to the parking lot together. There was still plenty of daylight for a mild spring evening, the blossoming trees still dripping from the day's rainstorms. In the winter, with daylight savings time, the story was different and safety in numbers was a good idea, considering our downtown location. Macy had referred to our block of old tobacco warehouses as *transitional.* She had assured us several years ago when we relocated from our midtown location that the area was gentrifying. Someday, it would be a great location for the office, she had said. I was still waiting for the gentrification to begin.

As we walked to our cars, I thought again of Mr. Evans and his weird little remarks about the power of the journal on the credenza. He knew my name, but no one was in the office except Jack, Stephanie, and me around the time he must have arrived at the firm and made his way to my office. "Hey, Steph, did Mr. Evans ask for me personally when he signed in this afternoon?"

"Evans? Nope, nobody with that name stopped by today. I always ask visitors who they are here to see and then note it in the book. I was at the desk all day except when I walked to the kitchen to clean out the coffeepot. I figured I didn't need coverage for my short absence since everyone but you and Jack was at the Chamber of Commerce function. Maybe he came in when I stepped away. What did Mr. Evans want?"

"Oh, it's no big deal, really. He had some reference material for the Norton-Grace project that he thought might be helpful. He knew my name, so I thought perhaps you told him I was in charge of the project."

"I never saw the guy," Stephanie said. "I wonder how long Mr. Evans was hanging around…and who told him your name."

Now, I knew Stephanie tended to be a little dramatic herself. She sometimes talked of conspiracy theories, too. Maybe she was suspicious by nature, but I could sense she was alarmed. Seeing she was growing upset the more she pondered Mr. Evans' undocumented arrival and departure from her lobby, I did my best to calm her. "Really, Steph, it wasn't a big deal. Jack was there in the office, and maybe he told this guy I was on the project. Don't give it another thought."

Stephanie nodded, and the frown disappeared. She was instantly absolved from guilt. "Well, as long as Jack was there, I'm not going to worry about it any longer. Jack could have told him who you were. I bet he even hung around just to be sure we weren't alone. I wondered why Jack didn't go to the Chamber event. Maybe that's the reason. He probably greeted your visitor in the lobby or something." She grabbed my arm and hunched her shoulders up in excitement the way some children do at the thought of chocolate ice cream on a hot day. "Jaaaaack is just awesome! He didn't want us to be alone in the office. How sweet!"

How sick. Drool nearly dripped out of Stephanie's mouth whenever she gushed Jack's name. If she were trying to hide her affections for him, she wasn't doing a good job. Yuck. It reminded me of the female drama from my sorority days. I guess some girls never outgrow the need for it. "Yeah, how sweet. See you tomorrow, Stephanie."

I watched as she got into her red econobox of a car before I drove out of the parking lot. I could guess who she was going to dream of tonight: her hero, Jaaaaack. If only she knew I'd be seeing him soon at karate class, she'd probably race to the dojo to watch him sweat through the workout. Stephanie and I were friends, I supposed, but her frenzy over Jack baffled me. He was just a guy who liked to flirt with every girl in town. He was what I call a *granola,* the kind of guy who rides his bike to work, takes little notice about his appearance—which is usually sloppy—and talks about moving to Seattle all the time. He'd fit in just fine there, I mused. He liked to camp and hike the nearby Blue Ridge Mountains, had pictures plastered all over his office walls of his time hiking the Appalachian Trail, and a blown-up image of him taken with his idol, the late Colin Fletcher, the iconic founder of modern backpacking and author of the classic guidebook, *The Complete Walker*. Ironically, only a few days after that photo was taken, Jack marveled repeatedly and often, Fletcher was hit by a car. He died six years later at the age of eighty-five from complications of a head injury he sustained in that accident.

When Jack joined Macy's firm, he told this story over and over so frequently that we all knew it by heart: he and Fletcher had met on one of Jack's many hikes in California. Jack was so impressed by Fletcher. Having read his many books and articles in wilderness magazines, which encouraged self-sufficiency on the trail, Jack begged a passing hiker to take their photo, and then paid the man four hundred dollars for his camera.

The one thing Jack and I did have in common was coffee. We were both coffee junkies, and Krankie's Coffee over on Third Street was our preferred supplier. Coffee… and karate. He joined my class a few weeks after he was hired as a civil engineer for Lachaise & Associates. He must have noticed the small photo on the credenza of me receiving my black belt from Sensei, so he started asking questions about the dojo where I practiced. So for a little over a year now, we've attended classes two times a week together, every Tuesday and Thursday. Stephanie's never known. Jack's gotten pretty good, though at first, he looked like a frog in a blender, his thin arms flying everywhere during practice. He would be tested for his orange belt next class. Tonight, the smaller children were going to be tested for their belt ranks.

My drive home to Ardmore was short. Ardmore is an eclectic section of Winston-Salem filled with bungalows, mid-twentieth century boxes, and a few Mediterranean-styled houses. I hated the word *quaint*, but that's what most people visiting the former working-class neighborhood call it. In more recent times, the grid-street neighborhood has been infused with cash from nearby hospital employees and doctors who want to live close enough to work so they can bike or walk there. It has a nice feel to it, and the new blood (and their money) have done wonders for this corner of the city.

As I pulled into the driveway, my large black-and-white cat, Chairman Meow, blinked twice, rose from his napping spot on a porch chair, executed a perfect downward-facing cat stretch, and sauntered over to *his* silver Mini Cooper to resume his nap on the hood as I shut off the motor. I call it his car because that's where he can be found when the car is in the driveway. I suppose he likes the view from the roof, and he relinquishes the car to me only when I slowly start to back it out. Poor old cat. He would be disappointed to be moved again in a few minutes after I grabbed an apple to munch and changed my outfit. Karate class awaited.

# Chapter Three

By the time I got there, the dojo was filled with eager parents talking not so quietly to each other as they waited for the testing to begin. They seemed nearly as excited for their children to earn new colored belts as their children were.

Sensei, courteous as ever, smiled and visited with each parent before class was to begin. After shaking hands with each mom or dad, he graciously bowed and moved on to the next one while one of several waiting teenaged students came along behind him and ushered the parents to seats along the wall so the center of the room could be cleared for students. The young students chattered like birds on a wire around the edge of a red mat with a large white circle printed in its middle. This mat was the stage, and the center circle was the equivalent of a spotlight where the testing would occur over the next hour or so.

Dressed smartly in white karate gis, twelve children, ranging in age from six to ten, lined up upon Sensei's command. When the room was silent, Sensei greeted the students with a small bow and asked them to sit down in a kneeling position. Only Sensei was allowed to sit in the single chair at the front of the class.

I took my place on the floor beside Sensei's chair, notepad balanced on my lap, as I also assumed the kneeling position. Thankful I was flexible enough to handle this kind of deep squatted position, I watched Sensei as he shifted in his chair. He didn't look comfortable, his big frame seeming to spill over the edge of the hard plastic chair. He'd often said that he preferred the mat with his students, but this particular testing time—a ritual of sorts—called for him to take a chair as the leader of the dojo.

Stroking his graying handlebar mustache, Sensei gave brief instructions for the entire class to hear. Slowly and methodically, he spoke his well-practiced speech. He had been teaching karate in this community for decades, and he truly knew how to put children at ease despite his brawn. "When your name is called, you are to step to the center of the mat. You are to repeat your name and address me appropriately. Does everyone know what that means?"

The class responded in unison, "Yes, sir."

"And what do you call me when you address me appropriately?"

"We call you 'Sir'!" Then from the far end of the room, where the youngest student sat, came a giggle and a joking reply of "We call you 'Santa'?" Peals of laughter followed.

Sensei stood. His 6'2" frame topped with white hair would be ominous for any criminal facing this active-duty county deputy of the Sheriff's department, but to his students, he was a gentle bear who could take the teasing as well as he could dish it out. He lumbered over to the smart-mouthed child, six-year-old Ashley Roberts, and got down on his hands and knees to be eye level with her. He got as close to her little face as he could without touching her and cocked his head to one side, pretending to be mad. "Do I look like Santa?" This brought even more laughter from the youngsters. Sensei tussled the little girl's curly hair. He sat back on his haunches and wagged a finger at her. "Okay, you can call me 'Santa'." He made a sweeping motion with his hand toward the rest of his students as he spoke to them. "But the rest of you must call me 'Sir'."

He stood up and resumed his position in his chair at the front of the room. "As I was saying, after your name is called, you will move to the center of the mat. You will state your name and address me properly. You will show me respect with a bow, but never, ever take your eyes off of me. You never, ever want to take your eyes off of your opponent, right?"

"No, sir!" replied the students in unison.

Sensei continued. "Once each of you completes your respectful bow to me—without taking your eyes off of me—you stand tall and be quiet. The rest of you in the peanut gallery will remain silent, too. I don't want to hear a peep; got it?"

"Yes, sir!"

"Talking while other students are testing shows disrespect. So does peeping," he added with a sly smile. Again, the younger students in the class responded with laughter, just as Sensei had intended. "Okay, let's get started. I will call out the forms for you lower ranking students. By the time we reach you green belts, you better know the forms in their proper order without me having to call them out to you. When we are finished, if you passed, then Santa's helper here to my right will decide whether you deserve a new belt." He pointed to me, and I played along by crossing my arms over my chest. "Shall we begin, class?" Sensei looked at his students with a stern face, then smiled again. He nodded to me to start the process.

From my place beside Sensei, I called out the name and current belt rank of the first student to be tested, who happened to be Ashley. Ashley stood and walked to the center circle of the mat, tentative in her stance.

"What is your name?" Sensei asked her, a broad smile on his face.

"Ashley Robertson, Santa," Ashley said stiffly, and bowed low to Sensei. She hesitated only a second before performing the basic forms of upper body arm movements and kicks with quiet prompting from Sensei. When Ashley completed her test, she bowed again and returned to her seat on the floor.

I jotted down notes on her execution of each step, and then I called the next child forward. As Jeffy Miller stood up to walk to the center of the mat, I noticed Jack saunter in and offer a quick bow of respect to Sensei. He was late, as usual. *Really,* I thought, *how long can it possibly take for him to drive from his place to the dojo? It's only a few minutes away. Most everything in Winston-Salem is a few minutes away! How disrespectful.*

"Blazer wouldn't start right away," Jack whispered in my ear as he kneeled down beside me, lining up the belts in the order the students were testing. His task in all this was to help hand them out at the end of the evening. This was a job usually reserved for the newest adult student attending classes, so Jack stepped up for the task. I gave a polite smile, which should have been a sneer, and focused my attention on Jeffy.

Jeffy was working on his orange belt test tonight, so it was expected that he could do better than Ashley, who was only testing for her yellow belt. That, plus the fact that he was two years older than her, was incentive for him to do well. When Jeffy offered his final kick and bowed to Sensei, I jotted notes as quickly as I could so the remaining students could get through their tests by the end of class. My irritation with Jack would have to wait until testing was over.

When his youngest students were through with the tests, Sensei rose from his chair in the front of the mirrored classroom and offered his congratulations. "I am so proud of all of you. Tonight, you earned the belts I'm about to distribute. Wear them proudly. Remember that each rank represents your commitment to karate, the respect you've shown me tonight, and the honor you've done for your family. Some of you younger students may have noted that those testing for higher belt ranks had to do more than you. You saw Alison and Mark as they quickly moved through the same forms you did at first, but also, they had to know more advanced upper body moves and kicks, as well as several katas, right? They have earned their brown belts tonight. Way to go, all of you! Give me a spirit yell!" Sensei urged them.

"Kiai!" the children shouted in unison.

"What?" Sensei's smile broadened. "I didn't hear you."

"Kiai!" they shouted louder.

"Better. Before you come in next time, I want you all to practice that kiai at home so you can do it loud like that on the first request. This means practice it several times a day, every day. I bet your parents would prefer that you do it outside, though. Understood?"

"Oss, Sensei!" All the young students cheered. Then they ran to Sensei, who stood in the center of the mat. The big bear of a man, who seemed gruff on first meeting, hugged each one and handed out belts as fast as Jack and I could toss them to him. Getting a new belt was akin to a party in Sensei's class. Laughter and hugs replaced regularly thrown (and hopefully blocked) punches and kicks. Sensei was well-liked and respected by students of all ages. That was clear.

Once belts were handed out, he called again for order in the noisy room. "Line up!" He turned sharply and took his place in kneeling position on the mat rather than in the chair at the front of the classroom. The students marched to their spots—in belt-rank order—on the mat, counting down from ten to one in Japanese. I fell in on the far end with the other two black belts in the class, both police officers, who knew Sensei best from his day job as county sheriff. *Yeah,* I thought, *this is one safe place to be.* I practiced katas with these guys twice a week and even sparred with them on occasion…or I should say they sparred gently with me, to my great relief. I'd witnessed some of the meaner moves they had heaped on each other in free sparring sessions, and I didn't want any part of it.

"Thank you all for studying as hard as you have," Sensei said. "You should be proud of yourselves. In this class, we practice Isshinryu karate. We are of one heart and one mind. In here, we know that the body is to be treated with respect, the mind is to be honored with solid, honorable thoughts, and the soul is to be treated to calmness as often as possible. We are to walk straight, speak the truth, and respect others. This is the way, my students. Understand?"

The younger students nodded in agreement, and several of them mouthed the words as Sensei spoke them.

"Next Tuesday, all lower-ranking adults are testing. For you three upper belt ranks not testing, come prepared to assist or spar with those who are. I'll post assignments on the website or email you before we begin Tuesday evening. If you're scared of the task I'm assigning you, email me." He smiled and looked directly at me, knowing that I don't really like to spar all that much. "For those of you who care to, you are welcome to stay tonight and suit up for sparring," Sensei said, before bowing and dismissing us for the evening. "Good night and congratulations to the rest of you."

"Come on, Lily; stick around and spar," Officer Tom Brothers called as he laced up his black foam sparring boots.

"Thanks, Tom, but I think I'll pass." A memory of the first time I stepped into Sensei's dojo flashed before me. In an instant, I was transported back to that day, timid and feeling like I had to learn to protect myself and my young son. We had come to Sensei's classes to have something positive to do together after we moved to Winston-Salem, and instantly, I had known this was a safe place to be. I knew these policemen who were suiting up nearby. And if I ever needed them for any reason, I knew I could count on them. At first, my courage came from them. They helped me—even without knowing—to get through a very tough time in life, a time when I didn't trust anyone. I barely trusted myself to make judgement calls on the people around me, let alone men. My ex-husband had given me every reason not to trust another man, and this class was full of them in the beginning. Now, as I looked around at them, I knew these men—these policemen and Sensei—were my friends. Here they were, again encouraging me to stay and spar.

I leaned over to collect my bag and fish around for my sandals in the heap of shoes in the corner, but I found myself executing a short upward block with my left arm in response to a heavy gloved hand on my shoulder. I caught Jack off guard with the move, and he stumbled backward a step.

"Wouldn't want to run into you in a dark alley," Jack muttered. "You really should stay. You haven't had a workout yet, and your reflexes are a tad slow," he teased me. "Besides, you've been sitting all day at the office like a mushroom and now here in the dojo. A bit of sparring will do you some good. Come on; I'll spar with you. I'll go easy on you, Lil."

"You'll go easy on me?" I snarled. "Well, I won't make the same claim." I quickly slipped on my pink sparring boots, shoved my mouth guard in place, and tightened my boxing gloves to show I meant business.

Three other sets of combatants besides Jack and me were facing off and prancing around the mat. Two police officers and two teenaged students were wailing on each other already, kicking at one another in good-natured fights. Jack took his time, poking and jabbing a little as I dodged his punches. I was just getting warmed up when I blocked one of his harder jabs and took him by surprise with a hook kick to the back of his knee and an elbow strike to his chest, which laid him out flat on his back.

The other teams of combatants stopped what they were doing and turned to watch as I dove on top of Jack, pinning his arms and legs so he couldn't move. "Know what, Jack?" I said in a low tone as I pressed my 5'4" body forcefully down on his 6' frame. "I hate to be called 'Lil'. Please don't forget that." I couldn't help myself: I grinned at him.

"I won't forget. Ever," he panted, and then he tapped my shoulder to signify I'd won that round of grappling.

The others in the room started clapping at my takedown. Even Sensei stopped his conversation with a lingering parent and turned to me with that sly smile of his. "I thought you didn't like to grapple!" He called to me over the others. He was pleased, given the light expression on his face.

"He made me mad enough, Sensei," I said as I got up off of Jack. I extended my hand to help him up off the mat and bowed to him. Then I prepared to go at him again by standing in the on guard position, with my legs slightly apart and my arms raised, ready to punch or block an attempted strike. This sparring thing was a lot more fun when I forgot I was scared to do it.

# Chapter Four

After karate class and an extra forty-five minutes of sparring, Jack and I walked out to the water fountain in the hall. He waited while I drank fully; then I returned the favor. I needed to talk to him, and I felt it would be better to speak with him away from the office—and away from Stephanie.

"Jack, thanks for the sparring. Glad you went easy on me," I teased.

"Too bad you didn't go easy on me," he said between gulps. "You're pretty good," he added, raising his hand to punch me on the shoulder. I raised my arms to block his blow, even though I knew he was kidding. "I mean, you're really good. I can see why you earned your black belt."

"I've been at it a few years, Jack. You'll get there. Just stay with it." I picked up my gear bag from a nearby bench and headed for the door. Jack followed. "You'll do just fine next week when you test for your orange belt."

"Does Sensei ever let adults skip belt ranks?" Jack asked quietly.

"No. Why?"

"Because I want to get my black belt as quickly as possible so I can whip you," Jack grinned.

"That will be the day," I teased back. "Seriously, Jack…you're doing just fine." This time, I was sincere.

Thoughts of Mr. Evans crept back into my brain. "Hey, I meant to ask you earlier: Why didn't you go to the chamber event with the others today? Wasn't there a big presentation or something?" I hoped he would say that he stayed around the office because of the late afternoon visitor.

"I had a phone call at the last minute. I was running so late after that, I just decided to skip the chamber meeting. They were unveiling plans for the new tobacco warehouse arts district with the developer, and since we're not on that project, I felt it would be okay to miss it."

"Did you greet a visitor in the lobby? Maybe about four o'clock or so?"

"No. I was still on the phone. I didn't hear anyone come in. Was there a problem?"

"More like a mystery. A fellow came in, apparently visiting us from Columbia. Stephanie wasn't at her desk when he came into the lobby, so he didn't sign in or have anyone to direct him to my office. Funny thing, though; he knew my name. I thought maybe you told him where to find me."

"I wish I had known there was someone else in the office, Lily. I was tied up on the phone the whole time.

Stephanie was back at her desk when I headed out this evening—maybe you need to check with her."

I played along as if I hadn't already done that. "Good idea. I'll check with her tomorrow." Then a thought occurred to me. "Jack, you started with the firm the month before Macy died." Speaking her name brought a lump to my throat, but I plunged ahead. "I remember we had just gotten the Norton-Grace project about that time, and we all went for a site visit and meetings with the Preservation Commission. Do you remember anything peculiar about that first visit?"

"No. Only that the place had been neglected for decades. The building was in pretty good shape, but the garden walls and pathways were a mess. The commission folks were great, just as they continue to be whenever I speak with them now. They showed such eagerness about what the place could be, despite its apparent state of neglect. Why do you ask?"

"Well," I started slowly as we walked toward our cars, "I was wondering if you remember meeting someone named Evans. He was the fellow who came in to see me today. He's not on the commission, and I don't remember meeting him in the gardens on any of the site visits we've done. He came a long way from Columbia today to meet with me, and he called me by my name. I was just wondering how he knew I was the project manager, and why he didn't leave his package with one of the commission members. They could have kept it safe until our next meeting."

"What was in this mysterious package?" Jack tossed his gear through the open back window of his ancient Blazer and turned to face me.

"Not much, really. It's a plant journal with notes from the owner—a young girl named Julia. Mr. Evans said…." I paused for a second, weighing how to say what was to come next. "He said the journal was somehow responsible for Macy's death as well as the death of one other person, and that I should take care."

"How? Macy had a heart attack. Was the reading *that* titillating?" Jack asked.

"Never mind, Jack." Now he had really pissed me off.

"I'm sorry, Lily; I just find it odd that her death and a plant journal could be related. I didn't mean to be disrespectful to her memory, or to you. Forgive me?" He gave a little smile that reminded me of a scolded puppy as he reached his hand out for a handshake. I bet he'd played this scene before. I wasn't falling for it.

"Just forget it," I scoffed and stormed to my car.

"Wait, Lil…I mean, Lily! I didn't mean anything by it!"

I didn't hear the rest of his pleading cries as I started my car and drove hastily out of the parking lot. When I looked in my rearview mirror, a slow smile spread across my face: Jack's Blazer wasn't starting. The dim headlights flickered as if they weren't getting enough juice from the battery. His happy-go-lucky attitude must not be loving *this* moment, but I sure was.

*Lil…Lily…*whatever. I said my name several times over in different tones to mimic Jack's voice as I drove away in a huff. *Why do I get so upset whenever Jack calls me that? He's the only one to do so these days, but it still bugs me. I've corrected him too many times to count since he joined the firm. I shouldn't let him get to me this way.*

It was a joke, really. My name was that of a lovely flower, a name that brought an image of something flowing, willowy, and full blossomed. Yet *Dahlia*—or Lily, as my family called me so as not to confuse me with my younger sister, Dianthus (she was called *Di*)—just didn't describe me at all. I suspected most women in this day and age would envy my 5"4', slender figure. I worked hard to keep it that way, with weekly karate sessions, swimming three times a week during lunch breaks when I was in town, and the occasional greenway trail jog, but I wouldn't consider myself willowy, beautiful, or even *pretty.* My hair was always a mess, no matter what I did with it. My nose was too big, sitting there between two smallish hazel eyes. My chin, well, "chiseled" was far too kind a description. And my disposition? It wasn't lovely, either. I could have blamed it on Pete, but I tried to hold myself accountable for my own feelings since we split. If I allowed my ex-husband to *make me* feel this way, he'd won. And I hated to admit I was a sore loser. Needless to say, *"Lily"* didn't represent me at all, despite my mother's best intentions.

To say my mom had a bit of a thing for flowers would be an understatement. When we were small, my sister Di and I delighted in fragrant smells wafting indoors through windows open to an overflowing garden that encircled our Craftsman-style home in the orderly Buena Vista section of Winston-Salem. While most of our neighbors treasured manicured lawns and tidy rows of flowers confined to beds like convalescents, our mother persisted in the belief that flowers, like children, should be free and somewhat wild, unrestrained and allowed to roam. And roam, they did. Trailing geraniums cascaded out of planter boxes fitted below windows. Heady white blossoms of star jasmine ran up wide trellises on either end of the sunny front porch, with its green wooden deck barely showing under terra cotta pots of herbs and potted tomato plants. Even the *haint* blue paint on the ceiling seemed demure compared to the hot pink fuchsias and bougainvillea flowing from hanging baskets. Smilax coaxed on nearly invisible wires festooned the archway of the porch, making the green front door shine like a bright peridot jewel in the center of an heirloom ring.

The flowers didn't stop at the garden, either. In fact, they graced every wall in prints and cheap calendar pages torn and displayed like treasures in gilded frames and on every piece of fabric on comfy furniture. My parents' home was a cross between shabby chic and English country cottage style…comfortable, cluttered, and welcoming. I was looking forward to going over this weekend to help with a project or two around the house, which generally meant a project in the garden this time of year. So far this spring, I'd designed and built rock gardens to help contain some of the chaos in Mom's gardens. I'd helped Dad with a brick walkway, too. This weekend's project was to finish off the remaining patch of grass: that area was going to become a water feature. It involved building yet another rock garden, which would accommodate a small waterfall and pond. Di had called earlier in the week to say she might be able to bring my two nieces over for lunch on Saturday, depending on the outcome of a soccer tournament for one and a dance recital practice for the other.

It would be fun to hear a house full of laughter again. Sometimes, living alone was a drag. I missed hearing the music Ben played in the evenings with his buddies in the garage during their high school years. They played diligently, the four of them, and even had a few gigs to keep them busy, but like many other things that disintegrated over the years, the band broke up when it was time for college. Ben still kept in touch with two of the guys. When he was home on college breaks, it seemed like old times, with music blaring from the detached garage that sat behind the house. Spring break might have been their last jam session for a while, I mused, as I pulled into my driveway and parked in front of the small garage structure painted to match the wood-shingled house with mustard yellow trim. I remembered humming whatever it was they were learning while I went about my garden chores. One song in particular they worked on during those practices jumped out at me: Van Morrison's "Brown Eyed Girl." It was a song older than any of the boys, but back then, they knew all the words. I'd have to dig up that song again to listen to it, now that it was stuck in my head.

Ben's graduation from UNC-Wilmington was a week away, and he was ready to go off to see the world. Literally. The 1981 thirty-eight-foot cutter rigged Cabo Rico that I got in the divorce and had given to Ben to live on while he was in college was loaded with provisions, new electronic gear, and a fresh set of sails, plus a bimini top in sharp navy blue to help him keep cool in the cockpit. Ben was ready to go, too. With a degree in marine biology, he was eager to put to use what he had learned. That, and he loved to be on the water. Much to his father's chagrin, I encouraged Ben to follow his heart and go sailing while he was young and unencumbered. Pete wanted Ben to be a man and get a *real* job, not follow his passion of chasing fish. I know Pete's always been a selfish bastard, and he really didn't care about me or the boat, per se; to Pete, my gift of the boat to our son was just a reminder of how connected Ben and I were, something he would never be. Pete has had little influence in Ben's life, and he hasn't been much help financially either through these college years, though he's had the means.

One more thing for Pete and me to fight about, I suppose, but I felt it was important for Ben to spread his wings and explore the world before he got caught up in an obligated life of job, mortgage, and perhaps a family at some point. Pete was usually up for a fight on the few occasions we had to be together—which thankfully were fewer and fewer, now that most of our *old* friends had passed the marrying stage and in many cases were well into the divorced stage of life.

Secretly, I envied Ben: he was doing what Pete and I had done when we were first married all those years ago. It had been such a lovely beginning, too, full of promise and adventure. Pete and I had taken a year to explore each other and the islands on *Windflower* after purchasing her and putting way more in to her than we really should have. We outfitted that boat with the latest and greatest gadgets of the day: sonar, radar, a first class radio system for Pete so he could continue to study for his radio operator's license, and a new computer system so he could search for work as our year-long sabbatical came to a close. I thought Pete hung the moon back in those days. He was smart, funny, attractive, and driven to succeed at whatever he tried. He yelled a bit as a captain, but I quickly learned to close off my feelings of inadequacy. I was new to sailing, and I assumed all captains acted the way he did. Other young wives complained of the same behavior whenever we gathered on beaches for barbeques and picnics, so I just shrugged it off. Pete taught me much about sailing, and even more about life. We were on top of the world when we returned from our voyage through several Caribbean islands. I believed things couldn't get any better for us as newlyweds.

Soon after our watery honeymoon, Ben came along. We moved inland to Greensboro when Pete accepted a position at a prestigious pharmaceutical manufacturer as a sales rep. It was a slow climb for him at first, but as he used the same charm on his clients that he'd used on me in our early dating years, he soon became the head of the sales team. Of course, our lives got complicated by Pete's job demands and the distance between Greensboro and the coast where we kept our boat. Before too long, the family sailing stopped and so did all the fun. Then the fights began when Pete's schedule changed to include later nights and overnighters.

Pete wasn't exactly discreet in his dalliances, so it didn't take long for me to find out about the young thing that soon became wife number two. I took Ben, moved home to Winston-Salem, and found a job where I could use my landscape design degree. I joined Macy's firm when my old firm was bought out by a bigger design conglomerate, preferring the smaller work setting that Macy offered.

Turning my car into my driveway, I smiled as I reminisced about sailing on *Windflower* with Ben when he was a child as often as possible, taking short sails around the sounds, and relocating the boat to Oriental when Ben was old enough to take part in sailing camps there every summer. One evening, after he had spent a satisfying first week as a sailing camp counselor at the tender age of fourteen, he shared with me his dreams of sailing the world...not with Pete, but with me. Even back then, I knew there might someday be a young woman who would turn his attention from me for such a sailing trip. Still, I promised him I'd do everything in my power to make that happen. Giving him the boat was my way of fulfilling my promise.

Now, I was about to see Ben set out on a new adventure of his own, I couldn't help but be proud of him, of the choices he had made the past four years. He would experience life unencumbered, debt-free. That was all good news.

The bad news? Pete and his *new* wife would be at graduation, too. Chairman Meow jumped from his spot on the back porch railing as I slammed my car door. "New wife…" I muttered as Chairman Meow responded with his usual chorus of meows. This time of the day, I interpreted them to mean "Pick me up and hold me." I did so, and he purred loudly as I carried him into the house. "Fourth wife. Or is it his fifth, Chairman Meow? I can't keep track." I put him down near his food bowl and was rewarded by his weaving between my ankles as I poured a glass of wine for myself and a bowl of milk for Chairman Meow. "Here's to fourth and fifth wives everywhere," I said to the cat. "Wonder how long it will take *her* to figure out what a jerk he is?"

Glancing in the refrigerator, I decided I wasn't hungry enough to eat much, so I popped some corn, grated cheese over it, and called it supper. Taking my bowl and glass to the screened porch, I enjoyed the growing musical rhythms of crickets and early peepers in the spring night. A persistent bullfrog joined in the chorus with his bellowing calls as Chairman Meow jumped on my lap once it was vacated by the popcorn bowl, making a furry mess on my karate gi. I must have dozed for a time because all was quiet when I awoke on the lounge chair. Chairman Meow woke me with his soft mew, signifying he wanted to go out to play. Obliging, I let him out and headed to the shower and to bed. Okay, so living alone wasn't so bad after all.

# Chapter Five

Friday at the office was quiet. The firm's loosely followed policy of warm-weather hours meant that Fridays could be half days, if work was completed earlier. I never got to that point of being able to take advantage of the half day, it seemed. The rule was a holdover from Macy's ideals on how a business should be fun and work should be balanced with playtime. She was great at both. Me? I could definitely handle the work part of the equation. The play part? Not so much.

Taking the afternoon off to play wasn't going to happen today, either. I spent the better part of the morning cutting a path through the clutter on my desk, making it somewhat more organized. The one thing I couldn't locate was Julia's journal. I had planned to take it home over the approaching weekend with other relics and reference materials on the project, but I couldn't find it on the credenza where I thought I'd left it the night before.

"Hey, Stephanie, have you been straightening in here?" I called to her over the speaker phone.

"No, Lily," she said. "I thought I might have time when I watered your plants earlier this morning. Your office was a wreck, by the way, but the phones started ringing, so I've been chained here ever since. What are you looking for?"

"Oh, nothing really," I lied. "I was hoping you were going to say you had time now."

"As soon as I clean the coffeepot out, I can help you for a few minutes. Looks like everyone, well, everyone but you, has already checked out for the day. And if it's okay with you, I'd like to leave right at one o'clock. I have a…a date tonight," she gushed.

The way she spoke, I could guess who the fellow might be, but chose not to. Instead, I urged her conspiratorially. "Oh, sure, that's fine with me. Who's the lucky beau?"

"Simon Hester, the architect on the Norton-Grace project. You remember; he was in for a meeting two weeks ago? Well, I ran into him at the grocery store last night, and he asked for my home phone number right there in the produce aisle. He said he's visiting his aunt here in town, and I guess we hit it off pretty well a few weeks ago at the luncheon meeting…."

I cut her off. "Come tell me all about it when you're finished with the coffeepot." I thought she would have more fun telling someone in person. "I'll be here whenever you're ready." I hung up and leaned back in my chair. Ah, Friday date nights. She'll enjoy her evening. Simon was a good-looking guy—and talented. A tad old for Stephanie, given that he was probably sixty and she was in her early forties like me, but she was eager to get back into the dating scene after her marriage fell apart. We've commiserated over the dearth of decent straight single professional men from time to time, but I never thought of her as *desperate.* Stephanie had a bubbly personality and an air of sorority-sister attitude about her that was hard to miss. I knew she had a wide circle of gal pals that she hung out with on weekends, going to the theatre or to the concerts. I also knew she had tried to draw me in closer to her side as a confidant on a few occasions. Her desire to share her excitement over this little attention from Simon was evidence of that. To each her own, I thought.

The design community was generally competitive, but historic preservation was a niche that only a few firms filled. Simon's architectural firm was dedicated to preservation and conservation projects like the Norton-Grace Mansion and similar projects throughout the southeast. Maybe he had another project here in Winston-Salem, so he decided to see the sights with a pretty woman like Stephanie. Can't fault him for that.

Just as she said she would, dependable Stephanie stopped in right after cleaning up the coffeepot for the day. Clearly in a hurry to leave, it didn't seem right to focus on anything but her evening. I waved her away from cleaning up the stacks on my desk and motioned for her to sit and tell me about her forthcoming date. She wanted to talk, so I listened.

"I got this cute green dress—we're going to dinner at the Fourth Street Filling Station—and then to a few galleries. It's First Friday, you know. All the galleries on Trade Street are open. You should check them out!"

"What, and cramp your style, Steph? Not a chance." I laughed. "I'm sure you and Simon will have a great time."

"I hope so. He's cute—for a man his age. Don't you think so?" Stephanie got up to leave, seemingly waiting for my approval.

"He seems like a nice guy, Steph. I only know him from our meetings and site visits together. Generally when we meet with the Preservation Commission, he heads indoors and I head out to the gardens. You'll have to tell me all about it on Monday."

"Oh! Gardens! That reminds me. Did you talk with Jack about that guy who came in yesterday afternoon?" The lilt in her voice betrayed her attempt to hide her anxiousness over her date with Simon. I guess she'd hoped that Jack would ask her out instead.

"I haven't seen Jack today."

"That's because he wasn't in. He called first thing this morning and said he had something to do today that couldn't wait until the afternoon. I wrote it in the log." Ever diligent Stephanie, covering for Jack again.

"Well, he has several projects going on right now. I'll ask him when I see him next week. As I mentioned last night when we were heading out the door, it's not a big deal." Wanting to divert her attention away from Jack and my visitor, Mr. Evans, I said, "I hope you have a great time tonight."

"Oh, I hope I will. I haven't been out on a date in a while. Frankly, I'm a little nervous. Maybe my luck is about to change." Stephanie flitted out the door. I heard her call good night on her way down the hall before I closed my door. *I* hadn't been out on a date in a while, either. Not that I minded. Much.

I continued to look through the stacks again for Julia's journal, then on the floor under the credenza, wondering whether it had fallen. Sitting down at my desk, I thought through the night before, retracing my steps with the journal before I left for karate class. I could have sworn I left it there on the credenza.

"Knock, knock!" It was Jack. He opened my door and slid into the chair across from me. "Looking for this?" He produced Julia's journal from his battered olive green backpack and carefully placed it on my desk. Before I could chastise him, he put his hand up to stop me. "Now, I know what you're going to say. I shouldn't have taken it without talking to you first, but what you told me about it before you left me stranded in the parking lot last night made me curious. Sensei helped me jumpstart the Blazer, in case you were the least bit worried. I came in here early this morning and found the journal, then went back home where I spent all morning reading it. And you know what I found, Lily? Absolutely nothing that was worth killing for. It's a diary of a young girl who has too much fun, if you ask me. She's going to parties, she's giving parties, she's going to dances, she's having dates, she's missing somebody, and she's digging in her garden. Frankly, it was a little boring. I couldn't even make it through to the end." Jack looked satisfied that he'd reported its contents so succinctly. He looked a bit smug, too. Maybe he thought he'd saved me from reading it myself.

"I'll thank you for not taking material out of my office without asking me about it first from now on," I said slowly, taking possession of the journal. "Anyway, I didn't exactly expect it to be a bestseller, Jack."

"Well, I wasn't sure what to expect…maybe a clue or something. I think whoever gave you this was just pulling your chain about that journal having anything to do with Macy's death." Jack sat back, obviously triumphant. He put his hands behind his head and slouched in the chair, looking a little too at home sitting there in *my* favorite comfy chair for my liking.

"I haven't read more than a few pages," I softened. "But from what I read so far, I'd have to agree that there's probably nothing important or *titillating* enough to die for." I emphasized the word Jack had used the night before as I shifted my gaze to the diary. I deliberately traced the jeweled "J" on the cover with my finger. "Why did you use the word, 'kill'?"

"Huh?" Jack leaned forward and put his arms on my desk.

"You said you didn't think there was anything in here worth killing for. Macy wasn't killed, Jack. She died of a heart attack, according to Dr. Tesh. Mr. Evans used the word, 'die'…you are the only one who used the word, 'kill.' Why?"

"Didn't you know? Julia Norton vanished. Her disappearance was never solved, and she was presumed dead. I got curious and perhaps a little nervous for you when I thought you might have something that could have led to Julia's disappearance and possibly to Macy's death. As I said, though, I didn't find anything mysterious *or* titillating in there." Jack pushed himself out of the chair and walked to the door.

"Jack, how do you know Julia Norton went missing?"

"I researched it online," he responded, pointing at my computer. "It's all there: archived newspaper stories and a page or two from a magazine featuring a socialite's column about her. That's what I was doing this morning. I was researching. Seems Julia was a popular young lady. *Very* popular. She came from a good family whose fortunes dwindled during the Great Depression. When the war began, her family did what it could for the war effort, and her father was rewarded handsomely by the city of Columbia for his ability to put people back to work making parts for airplanes. As the war came to a close, the family's finances stabilized, but Julia went into a tailspin over something. One article said she began turning down invitations to big parties after the boys came home. Another reported that rumors about a secret marriage made her go into hiding. Anyway, there wasn't anything about that in the journal. Just notes about parties when she was young, plants she liked…stuff like that was in the pages that I did manage to get through. Like I said, I couldn't keep my eyes open for the whole thing." Jack stood up and slung his backpack over his shoulder. "I don't think there's anything to worry about, Lily. Anyway, I've got your back, just in case." He started to leave, then ducked his head back in my office. "By the way, what are you doing tonight? There's a new exhibit at one of the galleries, and a performance at the School of the Arts worth checking out. Care to join me for either one?"

I was flabbergasted. Was Jack Chapman asking me out on a date? Recovering as quickly as I could, I answered slowly, "I have errands to run this afternoon, but I could meet you at the exhibit. Where is it?"

"In the Piedmont Craftsmen Gallery on Trade Street. A local furniture maker I admire has his work on exhibit there along with other craftspeople, and tonight is an opening reception dedicated to him with wine and cheese. The party is in conjunction with the First Friday Gallery Crawl, you know. This guy does amazing stuff with floating tops and tapered legs, the kind of work I dream of doing some day. I've had my eye on one of his neat hall tables for a few months now, and I'd really like to meet him. You may find something in there you like, too. How about we meet there at seven o'clock? Then we'll find something to eat, maybe at Sweet Potatoes. Does that sound good?"

I hesitated. Just last night at the dojo, I was throwing Jack around like a rag doll. And tonight, he wants to go to a gallery exhibit and dinner with me. I acquiesced. "I know the place. I'll see you at the gallery." What did I just do? I agreed to go out with someone I work with—a big taboo—and it's someone I'm not sure I even like very well. I must be lonelier than I thought.

"Great!" Jack smiled. "See you then." He waved goodbye and whistled his way down the hall.

What just happened? I looked down at the journal in front of me. Dismissing the jabbering little voice in my head which was going on and on about coworker dating no-no's, I shoved the journal into my already stuffed briefcase, turned off my computer, and left for the day, locking the front door as I pulled it shut.

• • •

Winston-Salem's Trade Street is lined with shops and eclectic galleries. Since this was the first Friday of the month, the businesses stayed open and hosted receptions for artists or hired an occasional musician to entice shoppers. First Friday, a brainchild of some wise marketing person intent on showcasing the city's incredibly creative side, helped drive people back downtown after work in warmer months to enjoy its artsy offerings. Other festivals and scheduled performances helped in this effort, too, and thanks to the University of North Carolina School of the Arts, Winston-Salem had shifted successfully from being known as an old tobacco town to one whose fortunes rested squarely in the arts. Recently, biotech and other branches of scientific study were joining the fray, so the area's demographics of old money and young artists were shifting to include scientists and more entrepreneurs as well.

The downtown's many former tobacco lofts were being converted into offices, research spaces, and swank apartments and condos. I knew Jack lived in one of them near Krankie's Coffee on a street that intersects with Trade Street, so I imagined his walk to the gallery district and its many offerings would be short. He was waiting just outside the Piedmont Craftsmen Gallery, talking with other patrons as I approached from the other side of the street. I used the parking garage one block up, buying a little time to compose myself and my freshly wrinkling Eileen Fisher outfit—pale silk top over charcoal gray linen pants—as I approached Jack. At that moment, I decided I hated linen no matter how good it looked on the rack. I stopped attempting to finger-smooth the wrinkles out long enough to raise my hand in response to Jack's wave of greeting.

"You clean up pretty well, Lil—I mean, Lily." Jack looked down at my open-toed sandals, then hurriedly back at my face, probably gauging my emotion to his mistake. "Sorry for that slip. I'll work on it."

"Uh, thanks. I think." I gave him a slight smile to show his offense was minimal—or at least I wasn't going to let it bug me tonight. I quickly appraised his cleaned up "date" style. He had skipped his daily uniform, which consisted of hiking boots, jeans, and a ratty-looking T-shirt in favor of comfortable-looking loafers worn without socks, light gray slacks, and a crisp white button-down shirt open at the collar. He rolled up the sleeves as we entered the crowded gallery. Instantly, I spotted Stephanie and Simon standing near a vertical display of blown glass vases. *This might get interesting,* I thought, as I smiled at Stephanie. A drink in one hand and the other clutching her small handbag, she clearly didn't look comfortable—or happy. Simon was standing near her, but he was talking to another woman. His body language was one of exclusion. That much was clear to me. Bet it was to Stephanie, too.

"Look, Jack." I nudged him in Stephanie's direction. "Stephanie is here with her date."

"Oh? Who is she with?" Jack was looking at the gallery's display of furniture rather than at Stephanie, so I nudged him a little harder in her direction.

"Simon Hester, on the Norton-Grace team. He's got his back to us, talking to the tall blonde behind Stephanie. Let's go show Stephanie some moral support." I walked purposefully toward Stephanie and spoke loudly enough to catch Simon's attention…hopefully to remind him of who his date was for the evening. "Hey, Stephanie! What a lovely dress! It matches this vase beautifully!"

Jack followed my lead and hugged Stephanie like a dear friend. "Great to see you away from your desk! How are you enjoying your evening?"

"Much better, now that my friends are here. What a coincidence." She eyed me first, then Jack. I could see the wheels turning in her head and hoped she wouldn't be too bent out of shape that I was here with Jack. I watched her face as lines furrowed above her eyes first, then relaxed as if to suggest her infatuation with Jack would still be intact on Monday. I watched as her hunched up shoulders relaxed, too.

"You both remember Simon Hester? He's visiting from South Carolina—says his aunt lives here in town." She tugged on Simon's tweed-covered elbow to get him to relinquish his interest in the blonde. He slowly turned around to face Jack and me.

"Jack, right? We met at the planning meeting, as I recall." Simon had his game face on now. "And Lily McGuire. So nice to see you again, my dear." He leaned in to give me a kiss on the cheek, but I backed away, making his effort more of an empty air kiss.

*How disgusting. You bring Stephanie out on a date, turn your back on her to schmooze some Nordic goddess, and now you try to give me a smooch right in front of her? Oh, no, you don't, Buddy. We're not on that good of terms.* Simon must have recognized the tainted look on my face because he backed away quickly and stepped closer to Stephanie.

"This is a nice place." He waved his hand around casually, taking the stance of a man who is comfortable at networking functions. "The building, in particular. Any idea what it was before it was this gallery?"

"The Piedmont Craftsmen Guild purchased this building in 2002," I answered, standing straight so that I was nearly as tall as Simon. "It was the old Pleasant's Hardware building. The gallery moved in after the space was remodeled in 2003. It's been a great space for them ever since."

"Sounds like you know the space well," he said, turning around to take it all in, with its open, beamed wooden ceilings and fresh white shelves stocked with a variety of glass, pottery, jewelry, and other objects of art. A caterer walked by with a tray of plastic glasses filled with wine. Simon grabbed a glass each for Stephanie and me. "Are you an artist, too?"

"Not an artist, just a supporter and admirer of anyone who appreciates *real* beauty and creative smarts." My small jab at his ignoring Stephanie in favor of the tall blonde was lost on Simon, but not on Stephanie. She smiled shyly to acknowledge my compliment. I meant it: Stephanie always has been an upstanding, reliable person at work. The few times I've seen her out around town, she's been *real*...not a social climber, as the Norse beauty seemed to be, pouting alone over there in the corner with her glass of wine the color of her bottled blonde hair, oblivious to the beautiful works around her. No, Stephanie was the real catch in this place. I turned slightly to Jack, who was nodding in agreement. He got it.

Simon seemed more intrigued with a particular table nearby. He moved closer to it and ran his hands over the floating top of golden curly maple, closing his eyes in apparent delight. "Have you felt this wood? Magnificent! It feels as smooth as silk!" Simon bent over to see the underside of the table. "Wonder how that works?" he asked nobody in particular. "Oh, I see; there must be a mechanism in here to hold it in place. Hmm, no screws or glue. Did you see this joinery, Jack?" Simon motioned for Jack to inspect the chopstick-like pieces holding the table legs in place.

"It's called a Torii table," Jack replied as he moved closer and got down on his hands and knees beside Simon. "The artist is a big fan of translating Japanese architecture into his furniture. This table is inspired by the Torii Gate in Kyoto, Japan. See those chopstick thingies? He's using authentic Japanese joinery to hold the table together. See, you pull these chopsticks." Jack pointed to the top of a chopstick sliver of wood. "The table comes apart, and the top slides off. I watched the guy who made it demonstrate at a craft show one time. The whole table comes apart for easy shipping. He's supposed to be around here somewhere tonight. This is his exhibit." Jack stood up and scouted around for the artist. "I think I would recognize him again if I saw him, but I'm going to go ask one of the people at the front counter to point him out to me." Jack walked across the gallery, moving effortlessly through the growing crowd toward the gallery's front reception counter.

Simon stood up slowly, continuing to rub the thin tapered walnut legs and tenderly touch the table's ebony accent line, separating the contrasting leg of walnut with a cap of brownish-red bloodwood. "I love it," he cooed. "I'll take it." Without even looking at the price of the table, Simon walked smartly to the front counter and whipped out his credit card in a flourish for all who cared to see.

"Decisive fellow, isn't he?" I muttered to Stephanie. I watched as her mouth dropped open upon seeing the price of the table.

"Yeah, decisive." Stephanie closed her mouth and regained her composure. Together, we watched a highly animated conversation between Jack and Simon happening across the room in front of the gallery's main entrance where sales were conducted. Jack's smile looked tense as he returned to us.

"That was the table I was going to buy tonight," he said under his breath when he got within earshot. "Simon bought it. Just like that, he bought it. He didn't ask to speak with the artist; he didn't even wait until I was finished talking to the person at the counter! He just swooped in, interrupted me, and bought the table I came here tonight specifically to buy!"

I could almost see smoke coming out of his ears. "Jack, is the artist here?" I tried to divert his attention.

"He was here a few minutes ago. The person behind the counter said he dashed out to his van to get a piece of furniture for another client."

"Fine," I said, gently soothing the approaching temper tantrum I've seen in men before. "We'll wait until he returns. He may have something else in his van for you." I hoped my matronly voice wasn't too conspicuous, but it did seem to help calm him down.

"This guy only makes a few of each table. It's not like he's got a huge showroom filled with inventory," Jack answered quietly, looking again at the table. Then he brightened. "Hey, look at that!" He slipped by a handful of people to stand in front of a bench with the same chopstick joinery pieces as the table had. "I bet…." He picked up the tent card on the bench and read the name of the artist. "Yep. This is his work, too." He sat on the bench, its long, knot-free planks of cherry beveled toward the center to create a slightly dished shape. "It's really comfortable." Jack jumped up and urged both Stephanie and me to take a turn.

He was right: the bench seat fit my own contoured backside. Leaning over the edge to look underneath the bench, I could see this one had the same kind of Japanese joinery, this time shaped more like wedges than chopsticks. Instantly, I started pondering whether it was available for use outside. I had a lonely spot in my garden at home that would be complete with one of these benches. For the first time this evening, I was pleased I'd come on this date with Jack.

"I love it; I'll take it," I mimicked Simon for Stephanie's amusement. Jack, on the other hand, clearly was not amused. "Really, Jack, I do like it," I assured him, "but I would want one for outside, if the artist makes them. You can have this one." I watched the color return to normal on Jack's face. I had no idea he was so passionate—or territorial—about art. Maybe it was a man thing. "Come on, Jack. Let's go see if we can find the artist. What did you say his name is?" I gently led Jack away from the bench so Simon would not notice it as he approached, looking triumphant at his purchase. I looked over my shoulder and stifled a laugh as I watched Stephanie sit down on the bench and spread her dress's skirt as wide as it could go over the bench's edges, as if guarding it for Jack. That a girl, Steph.

Jack looked back, too, and laughed. When he turned around, a woman behind the counter was waving to him. Jack walked briskly three steps to the counter where the furniture maker stood greeting other admirers.

I reached them just in time to hear the conclusion of the bench sale, and Jack was ecstatic. Jack shared with the artist his love of wood, and I saw the two were kindred spirits by the way they animatedly discussed how to care for the bench. Jack mentioned the time he had met the furniture maker at the annual Piedmont Craftsmen's Fair held in town each November. He was enthusiastic in tone about having studied the furniture maker's website, and he ordered another table right there on the spot. It was a grand purchase, too: an expandable dining table rather than the console Simon had purchased earlier. I left Jack and the artist discussing wood choices, sizes, and the various ways the woods could be combined as I wandered away from the counter and up the ramp to a second level of the showroom. Who knew Jack would want a dining table? I never thought of him as domestic enough to sit still at one, let alone have others over for a meal. But who was I kidding? I didn't know him at all. I saw that now.

The room was filled with a lovely soft light appropriate for a gallery, accented by spots of bright light poised on works of art. Jazz music drifted over the conversations of the artfully-clad patrons, some heads topped with felt hats and others with dreadlocks. An interesting array of art lovers and artists, no doubt. I had to admit, this was a lovely event. I had shopped in this gallery before, but it had been a while. I noted two wall hangings by a local artist similar to one I already owned. Beside it was an aquamarine-colored tapestry with flecks of green in it that, from this distance, looked like ocean waves beckoning. Drawn to the piece, I could see thousands of strands of silk thread were woven intricately to make the scene in the foot-wide work. A sudden wave of impulse—the kind I rarely feel anymore—washed over me: I *had* to have this piece. Quickly looking at the tag on it, I noted the artist's name as well as the work's title. Happy early Christmas to me…and birthday, and Valentine's Day, and every other gift-giving holiday for the next year, I thought, as I floated down the ramp to the sales counter to make my purchase. As I made arrangements to pick up the artwork the following week, I instantly remembered why I avoided this place for long periods of time. Buyer's remorse behind me, I smiled.

Standing nearby, Jack and the furniture maker were still going strong in their conversation. They were now talking about chairs and debating the merits of ultrasuede fabric choices. I couldn't help myself, but I started to giggle. "I never thought of you as the domestic type, Jack."

When the furniture maker turned briefly to answer another admirer's question about his work, Jack responded to my jab. "I suspect there's a lot you don't know about me." I watched him smile, then turn his attention back to the furniture maker. Jack offered him a business card. "I'd like to come to your shop and see the wood choices before committing. I can't make up my mind between the cherry and the bubinga."

The artist exchanged his business card and leaned over the counter to fetch a folded brochure. "Here are pictures of the different types of wood you're interested in, Jack. Just give me a call and we'll set up a convenient time for you to come to my shop in Mount Airy." Winding up their conversation, the two men shook hands, and Jack turned his attention back to me.

"I'm getting hungry," Jack said as he glanced at his watch. "Are you up for something at Sweet Potatoes?"

"I guess, if we can get in there," I shrugged. "I can imagine the place is going to be packed, though."

"No worries," Jack said, giving me his bright smile again. "I've got connections."

"I'm impressed you thought that far ahead. I didn't think they took reservations."

"They don't." Jack cocked his head to one side. "You don't really like me that much, do you, Lily?" He turned briefly and waved goodbye to Stephanie and Simon, who were coming down the ramp from the gallery's upper level. "Hope they have a good evening—it seems to have gotten off to a rockier start than ours."

Realizing how sensitive Jack was, I felt badly for my snarky comments. "Sorry, Jack. Didn't mean anything by it. Dinner at Sweet Potatoes would be lovely." I meant it. "You're right. It's wrong of me to make assumptions about you. I guess I don't really know you that well."

"Perhaps we can change that," he said as he steered me through the crowd to the door with a gentle hand to my back. "I may just surprise you."

"You already have, Jack. You already have."

# Chapter Six

Sweet Potatoes is one of those restaurants in Winston-Salem that diners remember and return to as often as they can. It serves down-home style cooking with a twist, with signature dishes involving sweet potatoes in some fashion: toasted sweet potato bread, roasted garlic smashed potatoes, sweet potato fries (my favorite), candied sweet potatoes, baked sweet potatoes, sweet potato pie, sweet potato cheesecake, sweet potato bread pudding, and sweet potato spice cake. The rest of their offerings are fabulous, too. By the time our table was ready, I had just finished another glass of chardonnay at the generous mahogany bar, which took up the first third of the small restaurant. Near the bar was a chalkboard listing the offerings of the evening, so I'd had time to consider my dinner options. It was going to be hard choosing.

True to his word, Jack did have connections. The fellow who greeted us at the door checked on us about the time my glass needed a refill and ushered us quietly past a few other waiting customers to a small table tucked in a corner. The patrons we passed by didn't seem too perplexed, though. It was still early by most diners' standards, and the liquid assets were flowing freely at the crowded bar.

Our talkative waiter greeted Jack like an old friend, reminding him how long it had been since Jack had last graced Sweet Potatoes with his presence (all of two days). I got the impression that Jack was a regular here by the way the two of them carried on. Connections, indeed.

"So, Jack," the waiter said, looking at me as he spoke. "You haven't introduced us yet."

"Sorry, my bad," Jack replied. "This is Lily McGuire. She's a landscape designer at the firm, and frankly, Wallace, she hasn't decided whether she likes me or not. I'm hoping you can push things in my favor. What do you recommend?"

Wallace the Waiter's smile broadened as I blushed. It could have been the wine, though. I'm not usually the blushing kind. I got over that shtick a long time ago.

"Well, friend, I can only help you out with the dinner suggestions. The rest is up to you. Or her. But I'll do my part." Wallace recited the menu without looking at anything. He assessed which chardonnay I was enjoying. Finally, he recommended the best thing for me was going to be the whole trout filled with sweet potato cornbread stuffing and wrapped in a neat package of bacon topped with crabmeat and a cold tomato caper relish. As if it weren't enough already, the whole thing was served on creamy stone ground grits with a side of greens. I couldn't disagree with him. My heart and arteries might be unhappy tomorrow, but I thought I could take this kind of meal every once in awhile.

Next, Wallace told Jack that the only thing he needed to order (in addition to another round of drinks, seeing that my glass was approaching empty) was the "smokin' ribeye," a barbeque sauce rubbed rib-eye topped with Jack Daniels sweet potato butter on horseradish smashed potatoes. "That way," he poked Jack in the ribs, "you won't much care if after dinner she decides she still don't like you." Wallace's laugh was infectious, and Jack laughed, too.

I did my best to suppress my laughter, but I was seeing a side of Jack I didn't know existed. He had friends outside of work. That was always a positive sign of a healthy person.

"And for dessert—in case you want to start with that first?" Again, Wallace recited the daily dessert offerings, reminding us they were made daily at the narrow restaurant. I declined, thinking the trout would be enough food for me, but Jack ordered a piece of sweet potato pie as an appetizer with two forks—in case I changed my mind. When it arrived along with round two of our drinks, I did try it, and was slightly envious of Jack's apparent metabolism.

"You come here a lot, I gather," I said over the top of my glass. Jack tucked the last bite of pie appetizer into his mouth and smiled.

"It's near home, the food is great, and I like the people here. Wallace is always looking out for me, you know?" He wiped his mouth with a linen napkin and drank from his water glass. "How about you? I bet since you're a local, you've tried all the places around here…or been to them with dates."

I sensed he was fishing. I didn't take the bait. "I like this place, sure. There are several great restaurants in town."

"Do you have a favorite?"

I only had to think about it for a second before answering. "My favorite place isn't in Winston-Salem. It's a place called Trio, and it's in Mount Airy."

"Mount Airy…." Jack reached for his wallet and pulled out a card. "That's where the furniture designer has his studio. Hey, maybe when I run up there to see this guy's wood for the table, we can stop in and have lunch or dinner afterward."

Oh, no. He's thinking in "we" terms already. Time for a diversionary tactic. "Sure, if my schedule is clear that day. This Norton-Grace project is somewhat consuming, you know."

"I know what you mean." Jack reached for a sweet potato biscuit. He didn't seem disappointed and dived right into the subject of work. "I was looking over the plans again this week to see if there's any flexibility in the schedule. It's really tight, considering the wet weather we've had so far this spring. It makes things challenging. I was hoping to get further along the project's timeline by now, but the commission folks don't seem too worried. Did you hear they want to add two more sculptures? They are contracting with an artist in Italy to re-create pieces to replace the ones beyond repair."

"It's a crying shame that two of the statues were destroyed by vandalism. Why idiots seek to trash a place like the Norton-Grace garden is beyond me. I mean, the efforts to restore a national treasure like that are Herculean! To think somebody thought it would be fun to decapitate two ancient statues and then shatter what remained boggles my mind." I was feeling the wine, and speaking my mind at the same time. I took another sip to regain my composure, enjoying the bright orange and black contemporary painting overlooking our table. The subject's eyes were so intensely vivid that I caught myself staring at the painting. "Sorry. I didn't mean to spout," I said, looking again at Jack, who seemed to be staring at me. "I am passionate about historic gardens the way preservationists are about old houses. So much life lived in that place, you know? It's as if the garden has a soul."

I drained the last of my wine just as Wallace presented us with another round of drinks. He placed them on the table with a flourish and swooped up the empty glasses in one fluid motion. Satisfied that he'd timed his task perfectly, he smiled broadly, bent down a little, and slapped Jack on the back like high school boys do at a basketball game. Given that he stood well over six feet tall, Wallace looked like he should be familiar with that sport. Standing straight again, he waved at two men entering the restaurant and motioned them to head to the crowded bar area. From his vantage point, Wallace could probably see his friends and patrons long before they made it to the bar, making everyone feel welcome. The bar was looking like a congenial men's club, and I had a ringside seat to the action. "Dinner will be ready in a while," he said to us before strolling away. "Enjoy your chat now, because when I bring those plates, your mouths will be busy doing something else."

When I looked back at Jack, he was studying me, smiling. "I believe you, Lily, and I agree. Vandalism is senseless and selfish. That's why it's up to us to give the place a proper makeover, to restore the garden's soul. Some say a garden is the keeper of the gardener's soul. In the case of the Norton-Grace property, I can see where that might be true. I can see your passion, Lily; I can see how much the Norton-Grace garden restorations mean to you. Have you had a chance to read any more of Julia's diary?"

I could feel a slight burning sensation creeping up my neck to my cheeks again. So much for being subtle. I was relieved to have something to talk about that wasn't me. "No, I plan to review it this weekend. Do you think the garden contains her soul in a way, Jack? In the first few pages I read, Julia seemed so happy, so full of life."

"I got that sense, too, Lily. She wrote of the house on occasion, but it was the garden that captured her thoughts, her imagination. She must have spent a great deal of time there."

"What do you suppose happened to her?" I regretted asking it as soon as the words slipped from my lips. To think that something sinister had happened to Julia, a young girl I'd never met, sent a chill up my spine. I recalled what grubby Mr. Evans had said about the diary, and I wondered what other secrets it held that he couldn't uncover. My thoughts drifted to other questions I had about Mr. Evans, but Jack's voice brought me back to the small cloth-covered table where we sat.

"According to the newspapers of the time, it was an unsolved mystery. Julia disappeared one evening. Her body was never recovered, but her car was. Seems she had just gotten a used 1941 Ford Super DeLuxe convertible as a birthday gift. Given the description in the paper clippings, it was a sight to behold. The newspaper article said she had attended a party at the home of one of the town's most respected families. Her car was found a few miles from home in a small patch of woods near the military base. There was no evidence of foul play, no clues, and no Julia. Another article written a few weeks later recounted the same story, and it added that her parents suspected kidnapping when they received a ransom note two days after her disappearance. They didn't report the letter to the police immediately because they were afraid Julia would be hurt. Julia's father said the note told him to bring a certain sum of money—something like $50,000, if I'm remembering correctly—to the local park and leave it in a hollowed out tree. He wasn't to alert the police, or Julia would be killed, the note read. Julia's father did what he thought was right. He gathered the money and put it where he was told. Then he waited at a park bench, just as instructed."

"What happened?" I moved closer to the table as I put down my glass. The wine could wait.

Jack leaned in conspiratorially close. "The article quotes Julia's father as saying he was knocked out cold. Someone hit him with an object on the back of the head. When he came to, the money was gone. He went home and waited for his daughter to come. After two days more, Julia's parents went to the police. I think it was probably too late by that point, though. The police searched for more clues and for anything that could have been used in the attack on Julia's father, but given what they had to work with at the time, they didn't find anything. They never found the girl, either. I read one last article that repeated all the stuff I've just told you, but it added an off-handed comment at the end that the police were ending their search. They surmised that it was just a case of a good girl wanting to elope with someone her parents didn't approve of rather than foul play."

"Well, I hope you two approve of the dinner!" Wallace interrupted Jack by placing colorful plates of food piled high in front of us. "Didn't mean to be eavesdropping, but that was a fantastic story you were weaving, Jack. Is this a new movie that's coming out?"

"Not really, just an old story I read that I thought Lily might enjoy hearing." Jack rubbed his hands together and smiled at Wallace. "You sure know how to treat customers right here, Wallace," said Jack, doing his best to put a stop to the intrusion.

"I'll take that as a compliment, Jack. Well, that's the kind of book I like to read. Murders, mysteries, just like what you were telling her about. Write down the name of it on your card, and I'll look it up later. Sounds like my kind of thing." Wallace sauntered off before Jack could reply. The look on Jack's face was one of amusement, though.

"Looks good enough to eat," Jack said, waiting for me to pick up my fork. As I bit into the trout dish, he got busy on his ribs. The explosion of flavors in my mouth captured my attention for the next few minutes.

"Perfect combination," I said after a few bites. "Want to try this?" Not thinking about possible implications, I held out my fork for Jack to sample. He took it eagerly and enjoyed the fish. When he offered to reciprocate, I shook my head. "This is going to keep me busy." I pointed to my dinner. "I might try that the next time, though."

"Glad to hear there might be a next time," Jack said between bites, giving me one of those smiles he gives out so freely. I can't imagine what I did to him to deserve this kind of positive attention, but I was starting to like it. The cynical side of me wanted to offer some snarky comment, but I restrained my tongue with another sip of wine.

"It was a good choice, the food, and the evening at Sweet Potatoes. And I'm glad you got to speak to the artist at the gallery, so that makes it a good night all the way around." I meant it sincerely, though I hoped I wasn't sounding too stand-offish.

"It's not over yet," Jack said. Then he winked at me. I swear he winked. I didn't think anybody did that any-more. Here we were, two coworkers, having dinner (and drinks…maybe too many), and he was winking at me? I could feel the snarky comments billowing up like fresh winds in the sails, but resisted. He's had a drink or two. Why shouldn't he feel frisky? That's all it is. Or is it? I sipped my wine and had another bite. Sultry soul music was piping its way overhead, and I saw more than one head bob at the table beside us paired with an occasional nuzzle to a close neck. Sweet Potatoes surely knew how to set the mood, and our neighbors were setting an example I really didn't want to follow.

I did, however, want to know more about the articles Jack mentioned, but I thought better of it. Best to get the night over with, so he doesn't hold out hope for more. "Jack, if you'd like more of this dish, you're welcome to it," I said as I slid the plate of half-eaten food his way. "Otherwise, I'll ask Wallace for a to-go box. I can't eat any more."

Jack held up his hand and shook his head. "I'm facing the same dilemma, Lily. We'll get them boxed up and be the envy of everyone we walk by on the way to the next place. I thought we'd go around the corner to Sixth and Vine for cheesecake after dinner. It's a short walk, but it will help move this stuff around to make more room for dessert."

"You had dessert already, remember?" I could guess where this was heading, and I wasn't ready for it.

"That was an appetizer, remember?" Jack answered. "Besides, it's a lovely evening, and it's fun to have company to eat with after a long week at work. Or...." Jack's smile disappeared instantly. "Perhaps you don't like cheesecake? They have crème brûlée and other desserts. And more wine...definitely more wine." He raised his glass to me in a toast. I relaxed and clinked his glass with my nearly empty one.

"I love cheesecake," I said, "but I'll have to skip the next glass of wine, or I won't be able to drive home."

"That would be okay, too," Jack nearly whispered. "My place is a short walk, and I have lots of room where you could crash for the night. I promise I won't make a move on you if you don't want me to."

"I don't want you to," I promptly stated. A part of me sitting somewhere below the beltline started to scream wildly, "I do! I do!" *Oh, shut up, down there.* Must be the wine talking. I needed to get some air, and a walk would probably do us both good.

Jack smiled at me, looking triumphant for the second time that day. "Well, that's a start. Off to Sixth and Vine, we go." He seemed enthusiastic as he waved to Wallace for the check and two to-go boxes. I could see why most girls would fall at his feet with these little teases and smiles he graciously offered. There was no sulk about him, no ornery mood swing, no pout for not getting his way. I had to respect and admire him for that.

When we hit the street, I wished I'd brought a wrap with me. Spring can be chilly or hot here in Winston-Salem. We often joked that if you don't like the weather, just wait a second and it would change. We popped into the parking garage and found my car so we could leave our dinner remnants. I also got an old cable knit sweater I always kept in the trunk of my car. The cream color didn't look bad with my ensemble, but the weight of the sweater looked odd atop the linen. I didn't care, though. It was warm. It hid a dozen new wrinkles in the pants, too. *Last pair of linen pants I'll ever own,* I thought, as we walked down Sixth Street to the small entrance to the wine bar.

"So tell me, Lily; what else do you keep in your car?" Jack asked as we sat down at the bistro-like table. A young waitress flitted over to take our order of a single piece of cheesecake and two forks. Jack ordered a glass of wine for himself, and the waitress waited for me to add my drink order. Water. Definitely water for me.

"I keep an old pair of boots, a few plastic bags for plant samples, a small shovel, and a few other odds and ends. They come in handy when I have sudden urges to stop along the side of the road to look at plants or collect a sample of a species."

"Do you do that often?" Jack sat back, looking amused again.

"Probably more often than I should admit. It's an addiction, I guess."

"And where exactly do you put all of your harvested finds?"

"Wherever they will fit in my garden. Sometimes, I find something that will work in my parents' garden, or in my sister's. We all swap plants. Hey, why are you laughing?"

And he was, too. "I can't help it, Lily. I mean, some families swap recipes, stories, books, or other stuff. Plants? That's the first time I've heard of that."

"And what about your family? What do you swap?" I sat back, too, matching Jack's position in the chair. This evening banter really was more fun that I cared to admit. But I at least wouldn't tell Jack that tonight.

"We swap furniture. My parents collect antiques, and my two sisters collect Danish and contemporary pieces. I have a mix of different styles in my place. I was going to buy that Torii table at the gallery for my sister for her wedding gift. She's getting married this summer, and I think she'd really like it. The artist said he could make another like the one Simon snatched out from under me before the wedding date, so it all works out okay. That's another reason for going to Mount Airy to his shop. He said he doesn't have a showroom per se, but he promised he would clean up the place for me if I just tell him when I'm coming to visit. Then we can talk about tables."

The waitress brought our dessert and drinks. Somehow, she managed to bring two glasses of wine with the water. I started to point out her error, but Jack shook his head.

"Don't bother. While you were looking over the menu, I motioned for her to bring two glasses, just in case you changed your mind." He must have caught the look on my face because he added, "Or in case I decide on a second glass."

I took a sip just to show my good-natured spirit, but I really had to pay attention because things were starting to spin a little. The cheesecake tasted good, but I feared I had overdone it with the alcohol for the night. It had been a long time since I had tied one on. "Furniture swapping sounds interesting, but that might get to be an expensive habit."

"We do it on special occasions. I mean, there's only so much junk and gag gifts one can buy. At least with furniture, it shows thoughtfulness, and the gift will last a lifetime. It's not something that's going to end up in the trash can next month. Plus, it's not as expensive a hobby as you might think, either. The table in the gallery is a special gift, but it's rare to spend that much. I like going to estate auctions and antique stores. Sometimes, I find really great treasures at the Salvation Army store around the corner from here. Not everyone knows the value of what's sitting around on the floor. Others just want to get rid of stuff because they have an attitude of 'dispositude.' That's what we call it in my family. That's where the treasures often are, in garbage piles, like on the Big-Item Trash Pickup days around town. You wouldn't believe what I've been able to find."

"And that's why you keep the Blazer?" Another sip of wine might help wash down the cheesecake.

"Exactly. You'll have to join me one pick-up day. Each expedition is an adventure. I never know what I'm going to find. So...when shall I tell him we're coming?"

"I beg your pardon?" I truly was lost.

"The furniture maker in Mount Airy, remember? He said he'd clean up his shop whenever I wanted to come for a visit, but that I would need to call first. You have your favorite restaurant to visit—Trio, is it called? I think it would be fun to do both on the same day. When would you like to go? Do we need to make reservations at the restaurant?"

Whoa. This really was too much. "Jack, I'm really beat," I said, getting up from the table. "Thank you for a lovely evening, but I think I need to head home. Now. Alone. Thanks again for a lovely evening." I could feel myself stumbling a bit. A brick wall of the restaurant reached out to grab me, but I held fast to the back of the chair I had been sitting in just a minute earlier.

"Wait; let me walk you to your car." Jack was flagging down the waitress and reaching for his wallet as he stood. "Maybe you shouldn't drive, Lily."

"No, no, I'm fine." I could feel my tongue lazily lolling around in my mouth, like it didn't want to work properly. Great. I'm drunk. With a coworker. With a good-looking man who might be interested in me as a person. I actually think I like this guy now. I'm definitely drunk. I took two steps and felt his hand at my elbow. I watched Jack place money on the table, and then I leaned a bit on him as the walls of Sixth and Vine closed in on us.

Jack waited until I gave him the keys to my Mini Cooper and helped me to the passenger side of the car. I protested once, then gave up and got in. Jack folded himself into the driver's seat, making a comment I am not sure I heard right…something about the travesty of little cars. As we were about to pull out of the parking garage, he stopped the car and gave me his big puppy-dog eyes look. "Which way?"

"Beg pardon?" Does he actually mean *your place or mine*? Can he be serious? It was one date. Or maybe that's how it's done nowadays. It's been so long since I've had a date, I didn't really have a clue how to respond.

"Which way?" he repeated. "I've never been to your home before. Where do you live?"

"Oh." I caught my tongue before it slid into a tirade. "Turn left here, then head toward Ardmore." I gave him the address and general directions. He seemed to know the way, so I resisted the temptation of being a side-seat driver. I truly was in no condition to drive, after all.

Less than ten minutes later, we pulled into my driveway. I'd left the back door porch light on, so it guided us up the three steps to the back door. Jack easily unlocked the door and helped me inside.

*Now comes the messy part*, I thought. "Jack, I really appreciate you driving me home, but…."

He cut me off at the pass and gave me what may have been the worst John Wayne impersonation I've ever heard. "No worries, Little Lady; I just wanted to see you safely home." He escorted me into my living room, turned on a light, seated me in my favorite comfy chair, placed a quilt over me, and patted my hand. Jack tipped his imaginary ten-gallon hat and said good night.

"Well, how are you going to get home?"

"Lily, I've hiked the whole Appalachian Trail. The few miles between your house and my place won't hurt me at all. Sleep well. I may check on you tomorrow, though. Night." He waved and walked back through the kitchen to the door. "I'm locking it on my way out," he called. I heard the door shut right before closing my eyes.

# Chapter Seven

A few hours later, Chairman Meow woke me as he jumped on my lap, hoping for attention. I adjourned to my bedroom, but I found I couldn't sleep after my early wine-induced nap. So much for a good night's sleep. After tossing and turning for an hour, I gave up and switched on the light. Julia's diary was on the bedside table. I found my place a few pages in and settled in to see what adventures Julia was having these days.

*I love it when I can spend all day outside in the garden. Never mind if there's dirt here and there on these pages; I brought my diary out to record the new plants I helped to put in today. I'm at my favorite quiet spot by the wall, the dappled sunlight filtering through the canopy of trees overhead. I feel so safe here. Safe from all that goes on beyond these walls. When I need time alone, to think, this is my place, my little garden. I can hear the splash of the fountain and sneak a peek at the walkway. Unless someone knew I was in here and came looking for me, I imagine he would never find me.*

Was the poor girl trying to hide, or perhaps she just had an overly active imagination?

*We were lucky to find such wonderful species on our trip to the coast. Mama says some may not make it in our garden, but I've taken extra care to amend the soil here to match the wet soil and swampy conditions that these plants came from near the coast. I loved visiting the beach. I was allowed to bring one friend to the beach this trip, so I brought Mary. My annoying little brother got to bring a friend, too, so for the most part, they stayed out of our hair while we were at the beach during the days.*

*We stayed at the fabulous Ocean Forest Hotel this time, and we saw the canal they call the Intracoastal Waterway. It was really busy, and we had fun watching all kinds of boats using it, like tugboats, sailboats, and a few other kinds of motorboats zipping along, sending waves to the sides of the canal. That's where I found these plants—inland from the beach. Some of them looked puny, but with proper care, they may make it. I noticed lots of activity near the Air Force base. I hear they use it as a base of operations for training and for the coastal patrols they do nightly. I noticed in the hotel room a printed card that showed the silhouettes of different planes. On the bottom of each one was a caption stating the type of airplane. A telephone number was printed on the bottom of the card as was a message instructing us to call if we noticed any of them while we were out in the evenings. Strange; I guess I never thought of being part of the war effort, but I would have done my part if I'd seen anything.*

*Mostly, though, we had a swell time. The Helleborus orientalis I found there look like they are going to make it. I can't wait to see their blossoms this winter and next spring. I love the way the deep green leathery leaves open to reveal clumps of cream-colored flowers that seem to be tinted in pale green paint. Best of all, I love how the blossoms turn purply-pink in the spring. It's like each of the little closed buds holds an incredible secret inside, and we gardeners have to be patient until they reveal themselves. Mama shook her head at me for digging up these plants, but it's been too long since we've been able to get fresh new ones, so I just couldn't resist. Besides, now is the perfect time to divide them, after they've flowered. Next year, the perennial plants at the beach will be even fuller, thanks to me! I never would take an annual or something I think has been intentionally planted in a person's garden, so I don't see what's wrong with selecting a few species from undeveloped areas. They are going to look lovely in my garden. I put them in a bed at the base of the fountain. They are fairly heat tolerant, so they'll be able to take the heat bouncing off the fountain's base. Daddy said the fountain was made by somebody called Hiram Powers. It dates back quite a long time...it was installed around the time of the Civil War, I think I heard him say. I like the way it looks, and often sit in my favorite spot imagining it in its former glory. Today, I've tended to the following lovely little plants.*

Julia's musings were interspersed with names of plants. Impressed with her knowledge of the plants' Latin names, I scanned the list that Julia included in the margins.

*Tradescantia sp.*, Spiderwort
*Iris germanica,* Common Blue Iris
*Hemerocallis sp.*, Common Daylily
*Canna sp.*, Canna
*Helleborus orientalis,* Lenten Rose
*Stokesia laevis,* Stokes Aster

Beside each of the plants listed on the page was a notation of numbers inside a set of parentheses, somewhat like an algebra equation. To the left of the *Helleborus orientalis* from the beach, in what looked like Julia's round and open handwriting, were the numbers "seven to nine." Interesting. I flipped back a few pages and found similar notations beside other plants. I gathered that was the number she hoped to salvage from her harvesting efforts. I liked this girl. She reminded me of myself, with her passion for plants and her notions about harvesting wild ones to add to her gardens.

*He stopped by to talk with me again today. I should probably tell Mama about him, but I wanted to handle it myself. A lady should have a say in who calls on her, Mary reminded me when I told her about his persistence. I do enjoy his attention, I admit. He seems so different from the other fellows who have come to call recently, but I wish he could call on me properly, the way they can. Mary says I probably shouldn't worry about that, because if he cares about me, he'll sort out how to act when the time comes. I respect her opinion—she's such a good friend. In fact, she's coming over this evening. We're going to the Mitchells' house for a party in her boyfriend's car! Mike got a 1940 Plymouth sedan that's in great condition. The color is battleship gray. With gas rationing these days, it's a very special treat to go for a drive, even though we could probably walk to the Mitchells' house. But Mike's daddy owns the farm out at the edge of town, and they have fuel for the farm vehicles, so I think he sometimes gets more than what others might be able to get due to the rationing. Mike is so lucky to have a car and access to the gasoline! He gets to go everywhere, anytime he wants. In fact, it seems everybody has a car but me. Sigh. I guess I better put up my tools and get cleaned up.*

Julia's journal entry ended for the day. I flipped through a few more pages and found her telling me all about the Mitchells' party: who wore what, what was served, and who danced together. Jack was right: Julia did like her parties.

A few pages more and I noticed her tone changing, or rather the words she used to describe things were blatantly different from words she'd used in earlier passages. Checking the dates of the entries, I found they were further and further apart, as if she forgot to write things down like she did at the beginning of the journal. I spent the remains of the night reading and re-reading her entries for signs of distress or something—anything that might have caused this shift in her writing style.

Feeling fuzzy from the evening's wine, I had a small glass of lemon-lime soda. I'd used this trick in my younger years without fail. Fingers crossed, I hoped it would work its magic again. Soon. On my way through the living room, I grabbed a notepad from my desk and headed back to my bed. Propped up with pillows behind me and Julia's journal in my lap, I listed the attributes I read in her entries to give me a better sense of who Julia was as a person. Putting them in chronological order, I noticed Julia was happy-go-lucky in the beginning of her journal. In her first entry, she was sixteen. She loved to go to parties, and she was observant of what everyone wore, who attended with whom, and what flowers were in bloom. The ever-present list of flowers in bloom running down the margin of nearly every page in the first half of the journal showed the changes of season by what was in bloom. It reminded me of an accountant's ledger, with each plant in bloom listed alphabetically in Latin in neat lettering. The lettering was so neat, in fact, it didn't look that much like Julia's handwriting. By comparison, her lettering was rounded and bubbly, just like her personality seemed to be in the beginning of the journal. She didn't always dot her "i's" or cross her "t's" when she made an entry, either. The handwriting on the side in the margins? Impeccable. It was almost as if someone else had listed the plants in her garden for her. Trees, shrubs, flowering plants of annuals and perennials…all of them were listed in the same meticulous way with a Latin name as well as a common reference.

**Trees**

*Quercus virginiana,* Live Oak
*Cedrus libani,* Cedar of Lebanon
*Cedrus deodara,* Deodar Cedar
*Magnolia grandiflora,* Bull Bay Magnolia
*Magnolia x soulangiana,* Saucer Magnolia
*Magnolia tripetala,* Umbrella Magnolia
*Juniperus virginiana,* Red Cedar
*Citrus sinensis,* Orange
*Citrus x limon,* Lemon
*Pyrus sp.,* Pear
*Prunus sp.,* Plum
*Ilex opaca,* American Holly
*Cornus florida,* Flowering Dogwood
*Magnolia acuminate,* Cucumber Tree
*Pinus strobes,* White Pine
*Gingko biloba,* Gingko Tree
*Paulownia imperialis,* Royal Paulownia
*Albizia julibrissin,* Mimosa/Silk Tree
*Ulmus Americana,* American Elm
*Vitex agnus-castus,* Chaste Tree
*Tsuga Canadensis,* Hemlock
*Koelreuteria paniculata,* Golden Rain Tree

**Shrubs**

*Prunus caroliniana,* Cherry Laurel
*Rosa laevigata,* Cherokee Rose
*Buxus sempervirens,* American Boxwood
*Buxus suffruticosa,* English Boxwood
*Chaenomeles japonica,* Japanese Flowering Quince

*Forsythia sp.*, Forsythia
*Kalmia latifolia,* Mountain Laurel
*Camellia japonica,* Camellia
*Hydrangea quercifolia,* Oakleaf Hydrangea
*Camellia sinensis (virdis & bohea),* Tea Plant
*Rhododendron sp.*, Rhododendron
*Philadelphus coronarius,* Mock Orange
*Azalea indica,* Indian Azalea
*Ligustrum japonicum,* Japanese Privet
*Yucca gloriosa,* Superb Adam's Needle
*Laurus nobilis,* Bay Laurel
*Jasminum nudiflorum,* Winter Jasmine
*Musa sapientia,* Banana
*Plantago major,* Plantain
*Artocarpus altilis,* Breadfruit
*Spiraea betulifolia Pallas,* White Spiraea
*Myrtus communis 'Compacta',* Sweet Myrtle
*Lagerstroemia indica,* Crepe Myrtle
*Punica granatum,* Pomegranate
*Buxus sempervirens 'Arborescens',* Tree Boxwood
*Prunus persica,* Peach
*Osmanthus fragrans,* Sweet/Tea Olive
*Ilex cassinas,* Christmasberry
*Rosa banksiae,* Lady Banks Rose

**Vines**

*Gelsemium sempervirens,* Carolina Jessamine
*Wisteria sinensis,* Wisteria
*Hedera helix,* English Ivy
*Lonicera sp.*, Honeysuckle

Watching the dates of entries, I noticed that the journal covered two years—two very important years in a young girl's life—with entries being made in the beginning as frequently as every week. By the middle of the journal, the entries were less frequent, but maintained what seemed to be a monthly schedule. At this point in the book, Julia's tone sounded less joyful and optimistic. She was seventeen, and I'm guessing things had changed for her at school, which I noted she didn't mention often. She still listed plants, but her comments regarding her social activities were terse.

*We are supposed to go there instead of Myrtle Beach for a change of scenery, Mama says. Mary isn't able to come with me, though. She made up some excuse, and I know good and well that's what it is—an excuse. She hasn't been the same since... well, things just aren't the same anymore. I saw them, together. I went to his cottage one night to see him. I heard her voice through the screened windows, so I didn't go in. Instead, I sat down under that open window, hidden by the azaleas. I listened to them talk for only an instant, and she was saying how happy the news was. I carefully stood up in time to see him present her with a jewelry box. That can only mean one thing: he loves her instead of me! I ran as fast as I could back here to the house. I didn't sleep at all, and I kept playing that scene over and over in my head all night long. For the last few days and nights, I've thought of nothing else. Today, when I saw Mary, I asked her if she had something to tell me. Well, the look on Mary's face told me everything*

*I needed to know. She is in love with him! It was as if she were hinting I didn't deserve a man like him, and that she was the one who knew his heart better than anyone. How on earth could she know? And why in the world hadn't she said anything about it until now? All the times I'd confided in her, she was keeping secrets from me. I tried to be gracious, and asked her to come on vacation with me in hopes that I could get the two of them apart until I come up with a plan to put an end to their romance. He's mine. He always has been, and I can't stand the thought of him with anyone else…not even Mary! But she said no to my invitation. She said she needed to stay home. I bet she's going to spend every second of the time that I'm away with him, and that thought makes me crazy! I have to do something.*

Hmm. Seems the best friends had a falling out over a man. I scanned the pages leading up to the middle point, reading again about Julia and her friend with the still unnamed mystery man. Last summer, Julia delighted in all that Myrtle Beach had to offer. In the remaining summer and fall entries, she had more parties than ever to attend or to host. Entries around Christmas seemed to be filled with tension within the family. This mystery man was still elusive. She never committed his name to paper.

Taking off my reading glasses, I rubbed my eyes and glanced at the clock. Great. It's four in the morning, and in just a few hours, I have a rock wall and water feature to build at my parents' house.

Deciding I'd reached a good stopping point in Julia's diary, I found a bookmark on my bedside table to mark my place. Turning off the light, I pulled up the covers and rolled onto my side. Thoughts of Julia kept me awake, though. Wondering whether Julia regained some sense of happiness by the end of the journal, I turned on the light again and donned my reading glasses. Clumsily, when I reached for the journal, I knocked it off the table. Collecting it from the floor, I noticed one of the pages toward the back must have torn from its binding: just a bit as it was jutting out of place. I decided that page was as good a starting point as any, so I flipped ahead.

The list of plants leaped from the margin to the middle of the page, along with the numerical notations looking like algebraic equations waiting to be solved on the side of each listing. The entries continued in their terse manner. Noting that Julia was now eighteen by the entries' dates, I read very little of parties, fine dresses, or friends. All the things she loved before seemed to vanish from her diary's pages.

*I saw him again today. I tried not to show how hurt I really feel, but this is just tearing me up inside to think he loves Mary instead of me. In all the time we've spent together, never once did he suggest that he had those kinds of feelings for her. Now that I think about it, he has been unavailable in the evenings for the last few months. I bet he has been seeing her all this time. What did I do wrong? I thought he was interested in me. I thought he wanted to be with me, but now I see how things really are. I'm so ashamed of myself for thinking about it this way, but I have to do something to make him forget her. I've made up my mind. I'm going to his cottage tonight to tell him how I feel about him. In the meantime, I will have to think up something to take Mary out of the equation so I can have him to myself—as it should be.*

Now, I'm no psychologist, but I had enough sense to see that Julia had spiraled into some form of depression…or obsession. In addition to her comments about wanting to be the center of this un-named man's universe again, Julia wrote of her plants in greater detail, noting their stems, the texture of the leaves on each plant, the number of petals of each and every bloom on a single stalk, the variations of color during a plant's lifecycle, and strangest of all, whether each plant was toxic in some way. Toxicity? What was Julia up to? Underlined in the journal beside each plant name on these latter pages was the type of toxicity, level of severity, and the results if the plant were consumed.

*Kalmia angustifolia or K. Carolina, a small perennial shrub with deep green leaves and saucer-like pink flowers ranging from nearly white to dark magenta. Toxicity: high.*

Now, I know the common name for *Kalmia angustifolia* is lambkill or sheep laurel because it does just what the name implies. The plant can kill grazing livestock. The laurel cousin is native to the coastal region of the

Carolinas. It can survive nicely at the beach, and perhaps as far inland as Columbia. Ingestion can be fatal, plus there are lots of other nasty side effects if it doesn't kill. The odd thing? In my tours of the old garden and a quick search of the commission's historical surveys when we first started the project, I didn't remember seeing this shrub listed as one of the laurels in the Norton-Grace Mansion's gardens. Mountain Laurel and Cherry Laurel, yes. Lambkill? No.

*Daphne genkwa, a tall deciduous shrub, erect branches, small clustering flowers in white, lilac, and pinkish-purple.*

Ah, the common lilac daphne. It's a pretty plant, offering the sweet lilac smell of a summer garden. But as with many other plants Julia singled out in her dictionary-like definitions, all parts of the plant are toxic, and ingestion is fatal. I'd have to see the copious inventory of plants assessed by the commission for this one, but I had a hunch it was not on the list, either. The commission had lists of all plants identified in the garden, as well as a notation for the earliest known records of each plant. This list of Julia's was something completely different.

The pattern continued for several pages, with plants listed in the same format. The common thread? All of the plants Julia mentioned in this part of her journal were potentially fatal if ingested. Her next entry dated a few weeks later struck me as strangest of all. It was written in the margins of the journal in small, tight letters. I had to get a magnifying glass out of my desk drawer to make out some of the letters. Clearly, the girl was in distress over something.

*I really shouldn't have done it. I know that now. But I didn't know what else to do. I'm so ashamed of how I acted. I know what he said, but I don't believe he meant a single word of it. He just wants to be with her, I am sure of that. I asked him where he has been going every night for the last few months, and all he could say was that he's been busy. I know who with, too. I should have left the room when he told me that, but I just couldn't bring myself to leave. Instead, I kissed him. I wanted to show him how much more I care for him, but he turned me down flat. My heart is breaking! I can feel it inside of me, shattering into a thousand pieces. I've made a decision, and I know what I have to do now. I can't stand the thought of the two of them together. I've thought this through carefully. If I can't have him, then she won't, either.*

Julia was definitely distressed—and sounding decidedly more dangerous, but was she distressed enough to hurt herself? Is this why she vanished? To get as far away as possible from a romance she couldn't have?

Given the dates of her entries, I noted that a few months passed between that passage and the next. Her tone had changed. Something darker was going on in that head of hers. The mystery man was her sole focus. There were no plants mentioned, only her thoughts about what had happened, but little about what she was planning to do about Mary and her mystery man. How could I have missed this entry on my earlier reading?

*The brooch…it just took my breath away. It's grand, with real diamonds and opals set in a design that looks like a flower. He had it designed especially for me. I can guess that he spent a fortune on it, too. I couldn't believe it when he said it was for me, since I saw him give a jewelry box to Mary, but here it was, in my hands. I held on to it for a second, then he put it on me. It was so lovely. His gift encourages me that he really does want to be with me after all. He told me about his night job at the military base, and about all the plans he has for us. I just couldn't believe it! But it looks like my happiness comes with a price.*

*I shared the brooch with Mary this afternoon. I wanted for things to go back to the way they were between us, with her as my best friend. I wanted for her to be happy for me, for us; but the look on her face confirmed that she is in love with him, just as I suspected. I bet she'll do anything to break my happiness—now that he's decided on me, instead of her. I want to be sure that Mary doesn't spoil it, though. I've trusted her for so long and counted her a friend, but no more. Things have to be different from now on.*

Julia ran out of room on the page, so I quickly turned it to continue reading what I hoped would be a full confession or at least a resolution of what happened. The other side of the page was smudged, but I could make out the list of plants continuing down the length of the page.

A few more notes scrawled in the margins as before were all difficult to make out. At the bottom of the page was a short note that looked as if it had been hastily written.

*Can't take this journal—it's too much of a reminder of everything, and I just....*

The last pages of the journal, however, were missing. Remnants of the paper held fast to the glue, indicating it had been methodically cut or torn out.

# Chapter Eight

"Why all the sudden interest in toxic plants?" my mom asked.

I'd been at my parents' home for a few hours, and as I helped dig the hole for the water feature in the back garden, I peppered my dad with questions about toxic plants. Weeding a nearby bed, Mom was as inquisitive as ever.

"I think I've told you about the historic garden project I'm working on in Columbia," I started. "Apparently, one of the home's occupants, a young girl, disappeared without a trace. She kept a diary, which turned up in my office one day. In it, there are lists of plants, some of which are categorized by toxicity, species, and location in the gardens surrounding the mansion. One of my cohorts on the project team thinks there's nothing to it, but…." I hesitated, knowing my parents wouldn't want me to put myself in harm's way.

"But you think differently." Dad finished my sentence like he often did.

I put my back into tidying up the hole I was digging. "Yes, I have been wondering about it. I wouldn't have thought anything more about it, had Jack not pointed me to old newspaper clippings about the girl's disappearance."

"Jack?" Mom pounced on his name, seizing it like a hope.

"A fellow at work. Jack Chapman. And no, we're not dating," I added. At least I didn't think last night counted as a date. *Did it?* I wondered. "Anyway, it might be interesting to add some of the plants back to the garden the way they were, at the time. The firm is thinking of different options to showcase the longevity of the garden and the importance of the property," I explained as I continued to dig, hoping to steer the conversation away from Julia's journal and Jack. No such luck. Mom held on to Jack's name like a life preserver.

"Never mind the history lesson; tell us about this Jack character!"

Dad and I unfurled the black pond liner and positioned it inside a berm, which was intended to keep runoff out of the pond.

"Oh, he's a character, all right. He's just a guy at work, nothing more. He's doing the civil engineering work on the garden's renovation, which has been attempted several times. It's hard to see the property in its current condition, knowing what it must have looked like at one time. Right now, the house commands the attention of visitors given the state of the grounds. The history of the property is fascinating. It's situated in a lovely section of Columbia, South Carolina. There are magnificent mansions around it, too. Some have had more attention paid to their gardens, leaving this one neglected over the years. There is a lovely fountain in place now, and there were statues that were vandalized. There are two remaining outbuildings, one of which is the caretaker's cottage and the other a greenhouse. Like many mansions of its time, the property is self-contained and somewhat self-sufficient. It's exciting to think the plans we've drawn up will showcase some of the different eras the property has survived. We are also planning on including new areas for children. It's going to be fantastic when completed."

Detour overruled again, Mom gave me the look I'd grown up seeing, and her hands-on-hips stance meant business: Mom wasn't going to take "No" for an answer. "Lily, you've been single and *alone* for far too long (as if I needed a reminder). If this fellow is decent, then by all means, go out with him!"

Stacking rocks like puzzle pieces, I covered the edges of the pond liner to hold it in place. "We work together, Mom, so that's that. I don't date people I work with." Well, not usually.

"Then quit!"

Seriously? This conversation was going nowhere fast.

Dad jumped to my rescue. "She's kidding; aren't you, dear?" Always cool-headed, Dad turned to me and said, "You're a grown woman. It's up to you to make your own decisions about romance and such things." I nodded my thanks to him, which he acknowledged with a gracious smile.

Meanwhile, my mother returned to her weeding. "Well, I just know that at *your* age, it's hard to meet decent people worth the time and effort required for serious relationships. I heard that on television. Just the other night, there was this talk show host—a doctor, mind you—who said the old rules of work being off limits for those looking for a date or a life partner were out of step with reality. Where else are you going to meet someone with similar interests than at the office? At work, you can see the day-to-day habits of coworkers. You can see if they are slobs in the way they dress, if they are diligent in their work, and how they handle stressful situations, for instance. All of these attributes are helpful to know before getting into a relationship. You should heed the good doctor, who by the way, has written many books on the subject of relationships. He's given talks all around the world, and is a huge success on the talk shows. Lily, are you even listening to me?"

Yes, I was listening. I was trying hard not to react, though. "Mom, I appreciate your concern about my love life. What I'm looking for in a relationship is the same thing I see in your relationship with Dad. So far, nothing else has been able to measure up. I've been in one truly horrible relationship, and that tainted my view on relationships in general. It's going to take a special kind of man to help me get beyond the hurt, and you'll just have to be as patient as I am. I don't want to rush into anything else."

"Rush? Lily, it's been years!"

She had a point.

"Okay, I'll grant you that. It has been years. But be patient. If a decent relationship happens in my life, I promise you'll be the first person I call."

"Well, I'll count on you for that," she said, somewhat begrudgingly.

"Lily's taking her time to find the right fellow, just like you did before you found me. What's wrong with wanting perfection?" Dad laughed.

I smiled, grateful for Dad's intervention. Sometimes, it's a slippery slope being best friends with one's parents.

Slightly deflated, Mom sighed. "Okay, okay. I'll wait for you to share such news when you have it to share. I think I'll go get lunch ready. Your sister and the kids should be here soon anyway."

Dad and I both agreed that would be a great thing—and a great diversion from this muddy conversation. While Mom headed indoors to start lunch, Dad and I turned our attention back to the task at hand.

I was careful to leave a gap between the stones so Dad could weave the pump's tubing and power cord through them. That way, if he ever needed to replace either, we wouldn't have to tear out the stones. When the arrangement met his approval, Dad used pond foam to seal the stones behind and below the slight ledge, which would create a waterfall. "This is coming together nicely," I said. My parents continue to teach and amaze me, even after all my years in this field of landscaping.

"Now, Lily, hand me that pump, please. Let's see if it works the way I think it's supposed to." As I handed him the pump, I glanced at the instructions again. Dad double-checked all the tubes and wires and placed it on an elevated set of stones. Once everything was connected, Dad stood up to admire our work. "Last step is to fill her up," he said, a satisfied grin spreading across his lips. "I bought corrugated tubing we can connect to the downspouts. The guy at the hardware store said he was able to fill his pond with rainwater in a few weeks."

• • •

Di and the girls showed up just in time for us to sit down to a lunch of pimento cheese sandwiches and fruit. I enjoyed hearing my nieces chatter on about the soccer game they had played that morning after the dance recital practices were over. I marveled at how my sister was able to keep their schedules straight, given that they often had to be at two different events at the same time most weekends. Between weekly soccer practices and dance lessons, I would have been exhausted by the time Saturday rolled around, but listening to the girls' excitement over every goal or header reminded me of how precious time with children is, regardless of the activity.

Listening to them reminded me of Ben's earlier years and gave rise to a small lump in my throat. My baby would be graduating from college next weekend, and I felt a mix of pride and sadness all at once. So as not to show emotions, I peppered the girls with questions about soccer, school projects, and other hobbies they enjoyed.

The older of the two, Nancy Jane, wanted to give me her favorite art project she worked on in class this week.

"I think you'll like it. I got an 'A' on it. Mama, may I get it from the car?" Nancy asked, her voice filled with the excitement that comes with being twelve years old.

My sister, Di, nodded and tossed her the keys. "We had such a hectic Friday after school, I left all their stuff in the trunk," she said to me. Turning to her daughter, she added, "Just be sure you lock the car after you get what you want from it."

Nancy ran to the car to fetch her award-winning project. When she returned, she shared her art with me. "It won first place in the art contest and was on the hall for two weeks! I want to keep the blue ribbon, but you can have the picture." Proudly, she handed me her prized piece of art: a medley of brightly-colored flowers displayed in a shimmering vase, complete with a shadow on the table in just the right place. An open window behind the centerpiece opened onto a landscape of green hills bordered by mountains on one side and a lake on the other.

I complimented Nancy Jane on her talent and commented on the serene setting of her painting.

"It's as accurate as I could make it," she said, beaming.

"I'll say," said her mother, frowning. "She carefully selected flowers from my garden, then dissected each one, petal by petal. She went back for more, and popped them into a vase just like that one to take to school for art class. Her work is extremely realistic, but my peonies are a mess as a result."

"Nancy, why did you dissect the flowers?" I asked, puzzled.

"I wanted to get the colors just right. Peonies are dark on the outside before they bloom, but inside, the petals are as pale as can be. When I looked way down at the base of each petal, the color was dark again. Besides getting the color right, I wanted to be sure I got the shape and the number of petals right for each kind of flower. Did you know there are odd numbers of petals for different species, yet all of them have the same pattern in each species? Like lilies have three petals and three sepals, which look like petals. So, lilies look like they have six petals. The patterns of three and three are a hint: three plus three equals six, so if I pay attention, I can see the pattern of three and six. Isn't that cool? I counted petals on several different flowers in different species just to be sure." She grabbed my hand in delight and pulled me toward the garden. "Do you want to see for yourself?"

Her excitement was palpable. Her little sister, Linda Jean, jumped up, too. "I want to dissect flowers. And bugs. Can we dissect bugs, please?"

"Best ask your grandma," Di said. "It's her garden."

Both girls looked to Mom and Dad. "Please?" they asked in chorus.

"One peony and one sample of two other flowers—no more, your choice," said Mom. "I'll get some paper so you can keep count of the petals." She excused herself from the table and met us in the garden, notebook in hand. "Here, Lily; you take notes." She handed me the notebook and joined in the hunt for the perfect collection of plants for the girls to study.

Just as Nancy had said, as she and Linda pulled and counted petals, patterns of numbers emerged. We kept score, and when the girls were finished, Mom brought out black construction paper and glue so the girls could create art with the petals as a keepsake of the afternoon while Dad and I finished the pond's construction.

"I'm so proud of your girls," I called to my sister. "They are as talented as they are smart."

Di raised her glue-covered hand in agreement as she helped the girls with their project.

"Maybe we have another couple of garden designers on our hands," Dad said.

"Or at the very least, a new crop of gardeners who really know their stuff," I replied. I meant it, too.

# Chapter Nine

Soothing tired muscles on Sunday morning with a gentle jog around my neighborhood, I tried to piece together what little I knew about Julia's family and her home life with the somewhat disturbing things I was reading in her journal. After a quick bite and a shower, I decided I needed to know more about the house. Maybe a clue could be found in its massive structure. A quick drive to work would soon dispel my curiosity.

When I arrived, the office was quiet, as it often is on the weekends. I liked being there alone, though I wouldn't admit that to Steph. She'd be crazy with nerves if she knew how often I came in to work on the weekends. *Alone.*

Sitting in my favorite chair, I reviewed the piles of reports and summaries of the property's extensive history in hopes of finding something of value. The mansion was built on eight acres of land in the north-eastern corner of Columbia. That was before the city was named the state capital, so few people were living in the surrounding area. One of the state's wealthiest planters took possession of it a few years later for a tidy sum of less than forty thousand dollars. The new owner and his wife got serious about improving the grounds. They also began transforming their "townhouse" into a manor home that matched its new neighbors, lining the unpaved streets of burgeoning Columbia. Soon, a married daughter by the name of Grace joined their gardening efforts, lending her married name to the mansion's property name, Norton-Grace.

Like other elegant residences nearby, grand-scaled gardens began to grace the area, with Palmetto trees mingling with India trees. Sometime around 1848, the family doubled the mansion's size and reoriented the house so its more formal side fronted Laurel Street. The surrounding grounds also got a bit of a makeover, with paths winding through gardens, tall hedges gracing certain areas, and formal parterre beds containing trees and ornamentals.

The lists of recorded plants were helpful to my job, but also to my interpretation of Julia's journal. I read with interest an invoice dated 1860 from a nursery documenting the purchase of plants, including asparagus roots, strawberry plants, cherries, apricots, and deciduous trees. There were also records of statues and fountains, including the Hiram Powers fountain Julia mentioned in her pages.

I had scanned many of these documents before, but I was searching for something that perhaps had evaded my earlier readings. There had to be something here that I missed, but I wasn't quite sure where to look as I combed through the volumes of material before me. The property as originally built had a privy, a kitchen, and a huge brick wall on three sides of the property. The last side, on Walnut Street, had a low masonry wall with an iron railing on top. Some years later, iron gates were added to the wall as an imposing entrance to the front of the house. There was a carriage entrance on the north-facing wall as well, and a nearly twenty-foot high *allee* of boxwoods defined the western side of the gardens. Other hedges of cherry laurel graced the Laurel Street side, and there was an accounting of cedars (both red cedars and cedars of Lebanon) in other areas of the early gardens. Crepe myrtles and English ivy also found their way into the literature, as did climbing roses on arched trellises, and wisteria in several locations.

A rose garden commandeered one corner of the grounds, and there were laundry lists of other species of flowering plants, trees, and vines mentioned in the meticulous records. In fact, many of the house records were clippings from newspapers through the years and an occasional magazine article from the early '20s that marveled at the grandeur of the gardens and its many structures.

Though devoid of all but one of them now, the grounds once boasted multiple greenhouses topped with glass containing exotic fruits or hothouses to help buffer tender plants from Columbia's winters. In my opinion, Columbia's weather always seemed a little warmer than I preferred, but with tropical and sub-tropical plants gracing the grounds, hot houses would certainly have been necessary. In the earlier dated records, there were also several buildings housing the primary kitchen, an office of sorts, a stable, and quarters for the help. A gatehouse, a caretaker's cottage, and a summer house were also mentioned in the records, but so few of these extra buildings remained that it was hard to imagine the self-sufficiency hinted at in the notes in front of me. Even the eight acres of grandeur had been whittled down over the years of encroaching development so that precious little of the garden area remained.

The property has indeed seen its fair share of uses through the decades. By the time my firm was contacted to help restore the grounds, it was not much to look at: a lot of grass and a few areas of scant gardens. The only garden seemingly intact despite its overgrown appearance was the one surrounding the Powers fountain. This was the one, I guessed, that Julia claimed as hers. The property had stayed in the family for generations, and Julia Norton was probably identified by her parents as the heir apparent who would continue the tradition of grand gardening, given her inclination for playing in the dirt as noted in her journal. Unfortunately for the property, it seems that soon after whatever happened to Julia took place, her parents sold the property.

Decades of limited use and fewer funds spent on it slowly took their toll. Clearly from the notes in my files, the projectile of demise couldn't have been any worse for the Norton-Grace gardens. Commercial development started to creep up to the historic district's boundaries, and little by little, the land from the original eight acres was sold to meet the demands of keeping up the manor home. Thanks to overzealous bulldozers used in earlier renovation attempts, what remained of the grounds was a far cry from what the documents in front of me showed they once were.

There was still a small greenhouse along one wall, and opposite it was a groundskeeper's house of sorts. Few of the massive hedges or grand trees remained, and the property covered only a fraction of what it once had. With the exception of the one fountain-area garden, a few traces existed of historic plantings to offer clues to the splendid gardens that once covered the entire grounds. It seemed the listings on these pages in front of me were there only as a forlorn memory.

I shivered to think what would have happened to the property had it not been for the push to preserve it. I had seen that happen to far too many grand homes and gardens in my years as a professional. I raised a silent prayer of thanks for people who can see the glory in what was before and who had the talent or the ability to raise funds necessary to save the property. At least I had something to work with in the garden, given these notes.

As interesting as it was, my review of the historic literature was not as fruitful as I had hoped. I reorganized the papers, journal articles, and notebooks and readied my office for the week ahead.

Gazing at my calendar before closing my laptop, I noted pending meetings for the week. A quick blink on my email alerted me to a note from Sensei reminding me of Jack's upcoming belt test along with his decision that I should be Jack's sparring partner. Great. *Something to look forward to,* I thought sarcastically.

• • •

The week started out as it often does, with soft-tipped bullets whizzing through the office halls and gales of laughter following cries of "man down!" to boot. A tradition that was well established by the time I joined the firm, this early-morning Nerf gun battle was deeply entrenched in the firm's corporate culture. Every week started the same, and everyone—including me—participated. If there was a hold out in the morning battle, he or she was bound to get clobbered in the afternoon session, which occurred promptly at three o'clock daily. On the occasion when there were guests in the office during either of what I liked to call our office-wide therapy sessions, bright orange and blue plastic guns were shoved into their hands when they entered the doors in the morning. Stephanie was the master keeper of the artillery, and she, of course, was extremely proficient at handing out the goods. She was also great at finding errant bullets that strayed into an unoccupied office, so there was always a stash of extra ammunition at her desk.

Today was no exception. I had just enough time to get to my desk and find my toy before my coworkers called me out into the hall for play. I had to admit, it didn't sound highly professional, but our special Nerf wars were certainly loads of fun. It was also an effective way to see who was in a good mood.

Today, I was in a good mood…for a Monday, anyway. The week was young, of course, and things could always change. And likely, they would. On my agenda was a continuation of writing pesky grants for various projects, plus a half-dozen or so mind-numbing meetings with clients who truly didn't know what they wanted, yet would complain bitterly that whatever plan I presented didn't meet their expectations. Sometimes, I hated this business of trying to please everyone for the sake of a buck. If Macy were here, she'd be able to coax out exactly what each client expected *before* I put pen to paper on a project plan.

I supposed the biggest thing likely to spoil this good-feeling morning of whizzing soft bullets at everyone around me was the thought of the approaching weekend. Sure, I'd get to see my son graduate from college, but I would have to face my ever-annoying ex-husband. That right there was enough to put a damper on anyone's mood—especially mine. With that in mind, I pushed all my hostility into my nearest victim, Jack Chapman, who laughed and cried for mercy before dishing it right back out at me.

"Hey, now, you're a bit trigger happy this morning, aren't you, Lily?" Jack caught his breath and waved his hand as if surrendering.

"This is what it's all about, isn't it?" I reloaded as fast as I could retrieve bullets from the floor.

Jack scooped two bullets up before I could reach them. "Okay; have it your way." He loaded and fired at me before

I could stand upright. Coworkers followed suit, letting loose on me all the ammunition they had amassed.

"Okay! Okay!" I yelled. "You win this round." I backed into my office and closed the door quickly. Stephanie may have had the main stash of extra bullets, but I had a hidden supply of my own…and a bigger toy gun in store for this afternoon's battle. I smiled a not-too-subtle smile at the thought of pummeling Jack again.

• • •

Lucky me. Sensei appointed me as Jack's sparring partner as part of his test for his orange belt in class Tuesday night. After the initial testing of his forms, which Jack presented to Sensei and the rest of the students in the dojo, Sensei instructed the others on what to practice. They were to focus on learning a new kata—a series of movements that, when flowed together, made an elegant but potentially deadly attack or counterattack during an imaginary fight with one or more assailants. Combinations of forms, including blocks, kicks, and strikes, were controlled in a flowing dance. At one point in history, katas were promoted as a way for karate masters to pass along their instructions to their students during the samurai occupation of Okinawa. Today, Sensei used katas as a means for gauging our understanding of flow as much as technique.

"Lily, gather your gear and follow me," Sensei said in a serious tone. As instructed, I followed him into a smaller room in the dojo to prepare for the one-on-

one combat Sensei wanted to see Jack work through to achieve his next rank.

"With all due respect, Sensei, may I ask why you've chosen me to spar against him?"

"Consistency," he offered, taking his seat at one end of the small mirrored room. "And practice. You need practice. This is one way I can ensure you're going to have it. As one of my higher ranking students, you must set the example for others to follow. Showing your willingness to sit out the sparring portion of our classes demonstrates that you're a sissy, and that's not good to show the children—especially the younger ones. If they see you walk away time and again from the fight that presents itself, they will naturally see that fear in you, and they likely will do the same. They will be fearful of a fight. That is not the purpose of this class. No, you need to get comfortable sparring so they will understand that, while fighting won't solve all our problems, it will sure take care of the more aggressive ones that may someday come after them."

"Thank you, Sensei." I bowed slightly to Sensei, knowing he was right. It had been a while since I thought about the example I needed to set in this class. I had become complacent, willing to ignore what needed to be fought: assailant, fear, memory. Whatever it was called, this dread I'd often felt since my divorce threw me back to the days when I knew Pete was cheating on me and I didn't do anything about it—at first. Pete must have seen that I was going to be a doormat that let him do what he wanted while still having his little family to show off at company picnics. Then he could pretend he was an upstanding citizen, a *good man* in the community, and worthy of the orders his customers blessed him with. When that bile-in-the-throat feeling of dread reared itself one too many times, I realized the example I was setting for Ben was so wrong: if I let Pete—or any man, for that matter—treat me poorly, then the only lesson I could expect Ben to learn was that women were willing to be treated that way. It was a painful time, but I extricated myself and took Ben away from that example as quickly as I could once I realized what I had been allowing. When Pete challenged me for Ben, I fought like a mother bear would to protect her cub. The judge in the divorce case quickly saw through the mask Pete wore, and I won sole custody of Ben. That bit of sparring with Pete took nearly every ounce of strength I had, but I would have done it ten times more if needed. By comparison, this sparring with Jack would be easy.

As one of the most senior black belts in the dojo, I should have expected to be called to this task. I suited up in my sparring gear under Sensei's watchful eye. We waited on Jack to do the same.

When we were both fully geared up, Jack and I stepped onto the mat's edge and he bowed to me. I returned his bow, never taking my eyes off my opponent. Taking two steps into the center of the mat, I stood in the on-guard position, ready for whatever Jack gave me. With a little coaxing from Sensei, Jack threw punches my way, which I blocked meticulously. He managed to sideswipe my legs out from under me in one move, though, and I was on my back. He hesitated only a second before he jumped down to pin me to the mat, but it was all the hesitation I needed: I rolled out from under him and pinned him from behind instead. When I pulled his arm behind his back, he yelped.

"Okay! You got me!" Jack sounded more embarrassed than hurt, so I let him go quickly and offered him my hand to pull him to his feet. I bowed to him, and he in turn bowed toward me. His eyes never left mine this time. After a few seconds of a stare-down, we went at it again. This time, try as I might, I couldn't get the better of Jack, and as I hit the mat with him holding me down, I tapped him on the shoulder to signify he'd won that round.

"Very good, Jack," Sensei said, clapping his hands. "I didn't think you'd be able to take her down, but you did just fine. Now, I have to go check on the other students, so you two keep at it. I've seen all I need to see."

"Thank you, Sensei." Jack bowed to him. "So does this mean I earned my orange belt?"

"I didn't say that. I said I had seen all I need to see." Sensei smiled that teasing smile I've learned to recognize over the years I've attended his classes. He was a sly one, our Sensei. I bowed to him as he turned to leave the room.

Jack threw his hands in the air, exasperated. "So what was that all about? Did I get my orange belt or not?" He reminded me of a little kid about to pitch a tantrum.

I played along for only a minute. "I wouldn't be too sure, Jack. Sensei can be very demanding in his expectations. Maybe he thinks you need another year of practice before raising your belt rank."

"What? Was I really that bad?" He looked petrified.

"You did just fine," I assured him. "This is just Sensei's way of making you want to practice harder. Now, get your hands up. I'm taking you down this time." I assumed my on-guard position again. For the remainder of the class, Jack and I went at each other in earnest. I couldn't remember the last time I had felt so liberated.

# Chapter Ten

Dread. Like a dark cloud, it hung over me as I drove to Wilmington for Ben's graduation weekend. Two sides of the same coin, I was glad he was finished with school and the tuition payments that had made my life uncomfortable for the last four years. Yet the flipside of that coin pointed to the emptiness my life would have without Ben coming home for occasional weekend visits. This was the trailhead for him, the beginning of his journey. The empty feeling of dread was compounded by the thought that I'd have to see Pete and his too-slim, too-perky, too-perfect-for-words wife, Elaine. At least that's what I thought this one's name was.

Truly, I thought I was well over Pete emotionally, and I felt wise for getting out of the toxic cesspool of a relationship when I had. That was the good news. The bad news, though, was that I hated being near him anymore. Over the past few years, we'd had to get together from time to time on Ben's behalf, or at a wedding, or more likely a funeral of a dear friend. Pete was still full of himself, as always. Sure, he was still charming, complimentary, and still physically attractive. Knowing him the way I did was enough incentive not to fall into the easy conversation he encouraged, or the dredging up of old memories he attempted as he always seemed to talk about the boat—our boat—the one I gave to Ben after winning it in the divorce proceedings.

And here, as I pulled into the driveway of the bed and breakfast inn where I would stay for the weekend's festivities, was Pete's black Lexus in pristine condition. I could tell it was his because it bore the sticker of the yacht club where Pete kept his sleek sixty-foot Riviera sport yacht, more boat than needed for his weekend cruises confined to the near-shore waters of Chesapeake Bay. But that was Pete: all show. That was all he was capable of these days, apparently. He paid someone to keep the boat cleaned and "at the ready," but rarely ventured out anymore, according to Ben. In fact, the last time Pete took Ben on a fishing excursion, Ben was just fourteen. Pete got terribly seasick, and Ben had to drive the boat through unfamiliar waters in the dark and dock it by himself.

Pete finally manned up to the truth on Ben's sixteenth birthday. Perhaps he felt obligated to discuss or share, man to man, what happened to our marriage and family. It was supposed to be a guys' weekend, and to my knowledge, it was the last time Ben went out on a boat with Pete. By then, Ben was completely at ease at the helm of any boat, regardless of size or type. He was also completely at ease with what Pete told him—he had figured it out on his own, long ago. It wasn't too hard after all: by the time Ben was a teenager, his errant father had repeated his habits and exposed his cheating pattern several times. Ben was wise beyond his years, even as a child. This was no different.

Ever the peacemaker, Ben didn't mention much about his father to me after that, not because he didn't want to include or upset me, but because they had such limited contact. After the divorce, Pete moved to Washington, D.C., for a high-level sales position. He promptly chose to join the *Dark Side* of boating, leaving sailing for the sleek powerboat he now owned and rarely used. I smiled at the thought of him morphing into a Darth Vader-like character at the wheel of his yacht, shouting orders to Storm Troopers on the forward deck.

• • •

Once I reached Wilmington, I quickly found my inn. Sitting in my car to collect my thoughts, I raised a silent prayer in hopes that we'd be on separate floors. I'd made my reservations months in advance. Then Pete made his. He felt it would be "fun" for us to all be together this weekend, so Ben could hang out with us and go to dinner in Wilmington's historic district. Ben had agreed that would be fine for him. I went along with it for Ben's sake, despite how repulsive I found the whole idea. Sure, this was going to be loads of fun. I could just see it coming.

Trying to keep my snark filter in place, I gathered my garment bag and purse before making my way up the front stairs to the inn's grand front porch dotted with white wicker tables and comfortable-looking chairs. Hanging baskets of ferns and pink trailing fuchsias decorated the open expanses between columns, a welcoming touch of Southern hospitality. I would have preferred to stay in Wrightsville Beach, but everything was booked well in advance of the graduation this year, which fell on Mother's Day. I felt accomplished for finding any place to stay this weekend, and I certainly could have done worse. In fact, there was precious little available by the time Pete got around to making his reservations. He must have sweet-talked his way into this inn, judging by the attractive hostess who greeted me as I entered the foyer. I could only wonder if he'd stayed here before. I wouldn't be surprised by anything he did, at this point.

"You must be Lily. Welcome! We've been expecting you," she said. "You're just in time for happy hour on the terrace." Holding a tray of glasses, she motioned to the hall leading to the back walled yard overlooking the river. "Come have a drink; then we'll get you settled in."

"I'd prefer to check into my room and freshen up first, if you don't mind." If I had to face Pete, at least I was going to look my best. And that might take some effort, given my hair in this humidity.

"Suit yourself," my hostess said graciously. "You're in room number four, upstairs to the left. The door is open and the room key is on the dresser. But you won't need your key while you're here. Just come on back down when you're ready. We're all pretty casual around here." She nodded toward the stairs and fluttered out to the terrace. Following to close the door behind her, I caught a glimpse of Pete standing a little too close to a curvaceous redhead who was *not* Elaine. She was graciously endowed and draped elegantly on Pete at a slight dip, the way a gentleman wears a fedora. I smirked at equating my ex-husband with the image of a gentleman as I climbed the stairs to my room.

Thirty minutes later, I waved off my gregarious hostess, who still encouraged me to join the other guests on the terrace, in favor of dashing out the front door to meet Ben at a local hangout between Wrightsville Beach and Wilmington. We had extended a dinner invitation to Pete and Elaine prior to making reservations at the Bridge Tender Restaurant, but Pete had declined, and now I knew why. Elaine was no longer in the picture. I suspected Pete was going to use this weekend as his "big reveal" of fiancée number six—or was it seven? In either case, Ben seemed relieved when it was apparent Pete wasn't going to join us at the restaurant. I could see it in his face as he greeted me from the outdoor patio overlooking the Intracoastal Waterway at the base of the Wrightsville Beach Drawbridge. Ben and I had enjoyed this place on many of my previous visits, and I was looking forward to the grouper Rockefeller I spied on the menu board as I walked in the door.

Ben looked incredible in his pale blue button-down shirt and khaki shorts. He had just enough sun glowing in his cheeks that I knew he'd taken an opportunity to visit the beach a few times during the last couple of weeks of school. He looked a bit like Pete, but more like me. I smiled at the memory of such conversations with Pete when Ben was an infant. Pete was so sure Ben would be a mini-him in manner and deed before Ben was born, but it soon became evident whose side of the family Ben favored. I tried not to gloat, but...well, a little gloating was a good thing when an ex-husband was so aggravating.

Ben hugged me as I approached the waterside table. "You look awesome, Mom!" I held on to him a little longer than perhaps I should have, but Ben didn't seem to mind or pull away.

"You too, Ben! I can't believe my little boy is all grown up and about to graduate from college. Just look at you!" It was true. Ben was a grown man, and he had done it without much interference from Pete. Now that was a blessing. We took our seats as I peppered Ben with questions about school, his exams, his friends, and his plans until our server came to the table to take our orders. After she left our table to put in our dinner requests at the server's stand, Ben and I talked about everything but Pete, and I was glad for it, too. It was easy to fall into our own little rhythm of speech, finishing each other's sentences, just as we'd done for years.

When our server brought our dinner to the table, I looked around briefly at diners seated near us. Several couples were with what I guessed to be their college-aged children, those who were about to graduate and join the working world. Other customers, mostly in single numbers, sat at the outdoor bar or watched a boater returning from an early evening cruise. Casting my eyes like a fisherman's net on the strip of brightly hued green marsh grass and to the waterway beyond, I saw we had a perfect seat for the evening. Streaked with ribbons of pink and orange, the sky made the lovely picture of springtime in a beach town seem complete.

There had been a few days, here and there, in recent years when I wished I were still out on the water enjoying sights like this daily. For a fleeting second, I wondered whether it was too late for me to go sailing again. It had been so long. Would I even remember how?

"So, how is it?" Ben nodded at my plate. His look told me he was hinting at more than just the food, though.

"The food is fine, Ben, as are the accommodations. Your father and I are not on the same floor. Have you seen him, yet?"

"Yeah, he stopped by the boat this afternoon for what he called a 'man talk.' There was something he wanted to tell me, but he couldn't quite bring himself to spill the beans. Has he got a new squeeze?"

I nodded. "A redhead this time." We both grinned and shook our heads in exactly the same way. Ben favored me in his mannerisms and build, but thank goodness, he didn't inherit my smartass gene. He's positively docile by comparison to me. "I'm glad to see you're not upset."

"Oh, well, I liked Elaine, and Jill and…what was the name of the woman before that? Never mind, they all seemed nice, but a little superficial or not too bright, if you ask me. It's none of my business, really. Dad can see whomever he wants to at this point."

I resisted the urge to spout something about the women Pete dated needing to be superficial to get along with him. "Well, this one looks nice enough, son. How was the rest of your man talk?"

"Short. I had just finished my last exam. Frankly, I was bushed. I was asleep below when he banged on the hull. We talked boats and a little about my plans, but that was it." Ben hesitated. "Mom, I've always wondered what you saw in him."

"The same thing that Elaine, Jill, and what's-her-name saw in him. He's absolutely charming, he's rich, and he's handsome. Still...." I promised myself a long time ago that I wouldn't run Pete down in front of Ben, either literally or figuratively, despite how I felt about the man. "Still, sometimes it's hard to be around him," I admitted.

"I get it," Ben said with a lopsided smile. "I'm glad you're here, just the same. Thanks for putting up with him and his new redhead."

"It's not about him this weekend, Ben. It's your time." I covered his hand with mine. "My little boy is all grown up."

• • •

Breakfast the next morning at the inn was plentiful, though I didn't savor it because the morning was so hurried. Frankly, I didn't want to dine with Pete and the new "what's-her-name." I rushed through my plate of baked eggs with rich remoulade sauce, and I weathered a bit of polite conversation with two other strangers at the early seating. I schemed that if I got to the graduation ceremony early enough, I might possibly avoid a confrontational scene with Pete. Unfortunately, luck wasn't with me this morning. Just as I reached the bottom of the stairs, Pete and the Curvaceous One, in a skin-tight leopard print dress that didn't cover much of her too-tanned legs, emerged from their room. She was giggling like a bubble-headed school girl, and he was trying to extract himself from her arms the second he saw me. Putting on a brave face, I waved and called a reluctant *hello* to the pair.

"Hello yourself, gorgeous," Pete responded as he lurched to hug me. His air kiss toward my cheek put an instant pout on his companion's full lips. "You look fabulous, Lil. Is your boyfriend with you?"

*Wrong assumption. Why you insist on abbreviating my name, I'll never understand.* "Hello, Pete. Nice to see you, too." If Pete were oblivious to the chill in my voice, he seemed even more so to his date, whom he neglected to introduce. I plowed ahead to cover up for him, as I had many times in the past. "Hello. I'm Lily, Ben's mother." Graciously, I offered my hand to her.

"Ben? Who's Ben?" the confused redhead squeaked in a voice not unlike fingers on a chalkboard.

At that very moment, I felt sorry for her. Either she was as absentminded as she looked, or Pete hadn't bother to tell her why they were coming to North Carolina. What a cad. "Your date's son." I glanced in Pete's direction. "You do plan on coming to his graduation ceremony today, don't you?"

"Of course," Pete recovered for his date du jour. "We had such a big time last night that I'm sure Tiffany here just forgot." The creepy look on his face was probably meant to make me jealous, but I was long over that act.

Of course she'd be a Tiffany. Her name suited her: light, expensive-looking, and high maintenance all the way. I had to admit, I did like her choice in shoes, though. I decided to give the poor girl a break. "So nice to meet you, Tiffany. I hope you'll enjoy your stay in Wilmington. Pete, the ceremony begins at two o'clock, and parking can sometimes be a challenge around campus so you might want to head over there early. I'm sure you already considered that."

"Absolutely, Lil. Do you want to join us? We can all ride over in my car."

"No, thanks, Pete; I have a few errands to tend to this morning," I lied. "Bye, now." I smiled and dashed up the stairs, struggling to avoid the temptation to take them three at a time. One meeting down, and potentially one more to go; then my interactions with Pete would be behind me for hopefully years—and clueless dates—to come. Why he still affected me this way was a mystery, but meetings with Pete always set me on edge. As I brushed my teeth, I recalled another such meeting at a longtime friend's wedding. I couldn't quite remember the name of Pete's date that day, but I'll never forget the way Pete made a point to call out my faults in front of her. He was smooth, though, covering the insults with laughs and slight jabs that an outsider—let alone a clueless date like the one he'd brought as his companion that day—wouldn't get. I knew what he meant. I let it get to me then. I wasn't going to give him the satisfaction or the time to do it to me this time, though.

Keeping up my lie, I left the inn as quickly as I could to avoid a second run-in with Pete and Tiffany. It would be good to plant my toes in the sand since I'd come all this way, so I drove to Wrightsville Beach. For a few minutes, I considered heading to the boat to see Ben on his big day before the ceremony. I thought better of it when I remembered that after our dinner last night, Ben said he was going to go see his longtime girlfriend, Claire. He'd most likely still be with her, and I didn't need to intrude.

I opted for a walk along the water's edge. Leaving my shoes in the car, I walked tenderly across the parking lot at the first beach access I could find. The morning sun, still white and rising, shined like a lustrous pearl on the gray sky. Clouds were giving way slowly, and soon the narrow strip of sand at high tide would be covered with early tourists with obnoxiously bright coolers and newly minted graduates. A freshening breeze tugged at my pale yellow dress, making it swell like a sail. The sand, still cool from reaching waves as the tide started its slow retreat from the beach, clung to my feet. The gentle small waves felt like an old friend's caress. How I've missed the ocean.

An occasional shell poked at my feet. Bending down to investigate, I found a nearly perfect Scotch bonnet.

That's what this day should be for Ben: perfect. I resolved to maintain that stance, even if Pete or Tiffany sought to ruin it in some way.

• • •

The graduating class was abuzz with excitement as name after name was called. When Ben rose to cross the stage, I clapped like a high school cheerleader rooting for my home team at an away game. Tiffany, who sat on the other side of Pete, looked at me for clues as to who this Ben character was. Pete, unfortunately, had insisted on sitting beside me. He looked smug and sophisticated until Ben shook hands with the university president. Then Pete went wild. He shouted, waved, and grabbed me. He planted a wet kiss full on my lips before I could thwart him! Right there in front of Tiffany, in front of everyone. Bastard!

What happened next was even more surprising: Tiffany's claws came out as she yanked Pete off of me, spun him around, and slapped him hard across the face. He deserved it, to be sure, but this was not the place for a domestic dispute. This isn't how grownups act, but perhaps that was the problem. Pete never grew up, so he kept on dating girls in over-developed bodies, like Tiffany.

I took the opportunity to move away from the ensuing harsh words he laid on her. Apologizing to my immediate neighbors, I climbed over a few knees to get to the aisle as quickly as I could. I'd wait until the graduation was all over, then find Ben out on the stadium field.

Hopefully, the two fighting lovebirds I left behind would calm down by then.

When the ceremony was over, I found Ben and his friends. Cautiously looking around for Pete, I approached Ben to congratulate him and to take three dozen or so photos of my young graduate with my camera.

"Have you seen your father, yet?" I asked as casually as I could muster. The plan was for us to go to lunch with Claire and her family, but I wasn't sure I could handle another confrontation with Pete and Tiffany.

"No, he called me on his cell phone to congratulate me and to tell me his date isn't feeling too well, so he wanted to run to the drug store to get something for her nerves and take her back to the inn."

I'll bet. "Well, I suppose I can try to change our reservations," I said as I reached into my bag for my phone.

Ben put his hand on mine and shook his head. "Mom, let's go sailing, just the two of us." Apparently, Ben was as conflict-adverse as I was.

What could I say? "Of course, dear, whatever you'd like to do. It's your day. Shall we wait for Claire?" I saw the lovely creature a few feet away, surrounded by her family and friends. Ben had spoken of her so often, and even brought her home to Winston-Salem a time or two. Claire seemed like a good match for Ben in many respects.

Ben looked over his shoulder toward Claire, then back to me. "She…won't be joining us. It's best for her to spend time with her family now."

"Oh, Ben. Did something happen?"

"We can talk about it later. Really, it's okay. I'm cool with it. I saw her at a party last night, and she mentioned that all of her family was in town for today's graduation. So, can we going sailing for a bit?"

"Sure," I said as I hugged him. "I'd love to." I called the restaurant to cancel our reservations, certain they would be swamped on graduation day. As I put my phone back in my bag, I looked up to see Pete and Tiffany heading our way and still looking cross with each other.

"Ben!" Pete called to get our attention, as if he needed to.

Oh, boy. "I'll go get the car, Ben."

"It's okay, Mom. I need to thank them for coming, at the very least." He stood up tall. "Hi, Dad," he called back to Pete. My peacemaker son turned to me and smiled. "You don't have to speak to him again, if you don't want to."

I stood as tall as I could, too. "I'm cool with it," I said, imitating Ben as best I could. Ben laughed and bent down to kiss my cheek. So sweet, this son of mine.

"There you are," Pete said as he pumped Ben's hand like a casino slot machine's arm. "I'm so proud of you. Look at my little man, all grown up to beat the band."

"U-hem." Tiffany's voice interrupted Pete's glad-handing.

"Oh, sorry. This is Tiffany, my…date."

I noticed a slight red mark still graced Pete's cheek. Good one, Tiffany.

Tiffany stepped forward and took both of Ben's hands in hers. "Congratulations, Ben," she oozed. "Your father has been telling me a bit about you this morning. I'm glad I *finally* get to meet you in person." She cuddled up to Ben.

The creep factor was starting to rise quickly, and I felt bile in my throat. She was probably only a few years older than my son, and she was coming on to Ben—right in front of Pete! Hell has no scorn, they say. It was going to be a long, cold ride back to Maryland for Pete.

Visibly perturbed at having a taste of his own medicine shoved down his throat, Pete tore Tiffany away, shook Ben's hand again, and stormed off toward the parking lot.

"Guess that means they won't be looking for us at the restaurant this afternoon," Ben said, stifling a laugh. "I'm glad you cancelled the reservation. So, how about that sail?"

# Chapter Eleven

Ben reached for a beer from the cooler in the cockpit's portside locker. "Want one?"

"Sure," I said, watching the horizon as a faint memory flickered into view. This could have been Pete and me, twenty years ago. Could have been. Would have been…was. We did this. We had our time. Now it was Ben's turn.

Patiently waiting with an outstretched hand offering me a cold beer, Ben waited for me to snap back to reality. "Hope it was a good memory." His lopsided smile was earnest, familiar, kind.

"I was just thinking of all the things I want to share with you before you start this next journey in your life." I gave my best *Happy Mom* smile, though I admit I was anything but. I was proud of Ben, to be sure; but I recognized what his college graduation really meant…and what his leaving to sail off on his new adventure really was. I was feeling it in my chest like someone had punched me hard when sparring in karate class. It hurt terribly. I ached all over.

"We've shared a lot, Mom, and I've learned a lot from you in the process."

I wanted to tell him to be careful almost as much as I wanted to tell him to go out and see all there was to see in this great wide world. I wanted to tell him to explore life before getting tied down to a mortgage, career, family, or whatever was going to distract him from *his* dreams. I wanted to tell him to remain strong and righteous in the face of temptations that surely would appear on his horizons, both near and far. I wanted to tell him how extremely proud I was of all he'd become, of all he'd do in his life...but I supposed he knew that already.

Instead, I offered only, "I love you." A simple phrase, but so full of life, truth, and meaning. I patted his hand and again looked to the sails, now full of the evening's early winds, full of promise of what life had in store for Ben as he took his boat—*my boat and my heart*—away with him on the adventure of a lifetime.

Ben took the helm again and we prepared to tack to bring the boat back toward the docks. He was pensive a long time before he spoke, and when he did, Ben's voice sounded hesitant. "I'm going to miss this place. I've grown to love Wilmington and Wrightsville Beach. I can see so many parts of life in this small area of the state among the students, the business people, the beach life, and the night life. I'm going to miss hanging out with Claire and Dale and my other buddies. Most of all, though, I'm going to miss you, Mom. You've helped me so much over the years, and I'm not just talking about the finances or paying for school for me. It's not just this boat, either. I'm going to miss our visits at home and our late-night talks on the phone whenever I've had issues with Dad or with Claire. You've been there for me. You have been my constant, my North Star. I know what happened with you and Dad was a long time ago, and I understand how much he hurt you. I see it still hurts you, Mom, even though you try to put on a brave face. I hope someday you'll find happiness again with someone who can be true. I know Dad's a jerk sometimes."

Ben chuckled at my look of mock-surprise. "Well, he can be! Even to me. I pray I remember never to be so selfish, or as arrogant with anyone as he has been to us."

My heart soared, finding its wings in Ben's words. I felt vindicated for some reason.

"You've been stoic about what happened, but I want you to know that it's okay to relax now. I'm grown, and I'm able to take care of myself. It's time for you to have some fun, too. You need to go have an adventure of your very own."

I smiled. At that moment, Ben appeared wiser than his years. In an attempt to avoid commenting on his statement, I asked, "Is Claire going to join you on your adventure?" In turn, he avoided my question and tended to the jib line for a few moments, tweaking the jib far more than it really needed, given the light air we were experiencing.

"Claire and I decided it would be best for her to find her own adventure." Ben cast his eyes upward on the sails as his voice grew lower. "We…we broke up a week ago, but I think we'll be able to stay friends. She's just not ready to set sail. She still wants to think about things, but she talks like she may visit me from time to time. She said she wants to keep in touch."

"She's scared," I answered. I knew exactly how Claire felt. A song quickly drifted into my mind, about living out on the edges of a bell-shaped curve, which is where Ben was heading. Claire came for a visit, but she lost her nerve. That was me, too. As the song by David Wilcox said, I had a hungry soul but a cautious mind, and I couldn't quite leave my world behind. And now, Ben was going to leave Claire—and me—behind. I looked away quickly so he wouldn't see me brush a stray tear from my cheek. My move was unsuccessful, and Ben hugged my shoulders with one strong arm. "It's going to be fine. Promise."

We sailed in silence for a bit; then Ben spoke in an upbeat way of what he had learned in school and what he hoped to accomplish in his first assignment working as a research assistant for the Reef Check Foundation. By the time we docked the boat, my energy was restored by Ben's enthusiasm for what was ahead of him. How could I not be excited (and a tiny bit jealous) about what came next for him?

Ben was set on a fulfilling career path where he could follow his passion in a way he wanted to and still make a decent living with a respectable organization. That's success, in anyone's book. For that, I was justifiably thrilled, relieved, and happy. I would always worry about him, no matter his age, his location, or his successes. Ben would always be in my every thought. Now that he was ready to claim his role as a college graduate and adult with this take-on-the-world attitude, I supposed I could relax a little. In many respects, we had been living separate lives while he was in college, so the empty nest syndrome so many of my peers fear wasn't new to me. I had my work, my plants, and my books. I did wonder, though, as I flaked the mainsail loosely on top of the boom, whether that was going to be enough for me. Maybe Ben was right. Maybe it was time for an adventure. But what kind? *Let's not think it to death. I'm always the one with a plan. Maybe I should heed my son's words and relax a little, and just go with the flow.*

Tied securely to the dock, my old boat never looked better. She had a new coat of paint, a fresh set of sails, and a guy at her helm who really knew how to keep her in great shape. Ben fussed about needing a new inverter as we surveyed the cabin.

"I want to show you something, Mom." Ben reached for a framed photo of a Nautilus shell. There were two images of the shell, one placed above the other in the small frame. "See this? It's one of my favorites. The nautilus who lives in shells like this is a cephalopod, a type of mollusk. It's the same scientific family as an octopus. The nautilus makes the chambers by secreting the substance for its shell as it grows, and it lives in the largest chamber it produces. When it feels a threat of any kind, the nautilus hides in the last chamber. It covers the opening with a secretion that toughens up like a hide. Can you see how the shell could continue in its spiral, with chambers that are larger, yet always the same?"

"I think I feel a lesson coming on," I said. "Am I the octopus or the shell?"

Ben laughed. "You're the octopus, but instead of living in this larger part of the shell where you can continue to grow, you seem stuck way back inside one of these smaller chambers. It's time to explore, Mom. It's time for you to see what else life—the shell, in this metaphor—has to offer. You still keep what's yours, but you can move on, now." Ben carefully placed the photo back on the wall. I could see he was indeed wiser than his years.

"Thanks for the lesson, professor; I'll keep it in mind." I would, too. I'd been living inside this small section of a shell for a long time now. "Glad to see you learned your stuff well enough in all those marine biology classes. I can now say I feel like I got my money's worth."

Ben smiled and offered me another beer, which I declined as I tried my best to tame my wild hair. "It suits you, ya know," he said. "I like your hair short."

"Thanks, son, and I like yours." I gestured to his wild every-which-way hair, "looks fabulous, too." We had a good laugh and hopped off the boat for a round of hugs. "Go play with your friends, Ben. Be safe, and write when you can. I want to hear all about your adventure."

"And I want to hear all about yours," Ben said. "Promise me you'll find one." Again, his earnest eyes and lopsided grin were hard to resist. Claire was an idiot, I thought, for not wanting to sail off into the sunset with Ben. Secretly, I wished it could be me sailing off again. I just nodded and replied something vague about the nature of adventures.

After the last of our hugs and final rounds of good-byes, I watched Ben drive back toward Wrightsville Beach to catch up with friends. I knew he'd be okay. As for myself, I wasn't so sure. Standing in the marina's parking lot, I cried, not caring who saw the crazy lady with the wild hair. I let it go full on, this torrent of tears, until it gave way to a feeling of complete and utter exhaustion. Walking in the fading sunlight to my car, I wiped away the remnants of my personal storm.

*Adventure, whatever you are, here I come. Right after I make a plan for surviving you.*

• • •

Pulling away from the inn the next morning, I felt lighter and heavier at the same time, if that were possible. My grown son would be pulling away from the dock in a few hours, and I resisted the urge to race back to the marina to hug him one last time. This was his big day, and his friends were promising—or threatening—a really big sendoff celebration. Most likely, he would prefer to slip away quietly from the dock to start out like he told me he wanted to: leaving on his own terms before his friends woke up from their hangovers, beginning as he wanted to, without all that fanfare. Ben had such a big heart, though, that I knew he wouldn't want to let his friends down.

After a quick stop in a local coffee shop for a double shot of enthusiasm with a side helping of courage, I started the long drive home. As I drove, I thought about Julia, driving away from a last party toward something—unknown, unplanned, or undecided. I could relate to what perhaps was indecision on her part. Maybe it was a twinge of fear she was feeling. Thinking back over her journal entries, I wondered what had made her change so drastically from a gentle free spirit to the haunted one on the latter pages of her diary. I recalled what Jack told me of the newspaper clippings he'd read, and I tried to piece it together. Party girl goes missing, never to be heard from again. Something didn't make sense to me, though. Why would a popular young woman leave her home if she hadn't been under duress? Had she been kidnapped? Or did she feel she had to leave? Jack still insisted the diary was a waste of time, yet the week before, on a daily basis, he'd popped his head in my office door to ask a question or two about it: "Tell me the plant names again," or "Why toxins?" or "What happened to the last pages?" Jack swore he didn't tear them out, but he also couldn't remember reading them either. He confessed he hadn't read Julia's journal as closely as I had, so I suppose he could be believed. As least in this matter.

I gave him credit for one thing: at least Jack Chapman was persistent. He had asked me several times over the course of the week before I headed to Ben's graduation to go with him to Mount Airy to visit the furniture maker. I finally acquiesced, and we planned to go this coming week after I sorted out some of the grants I was working on for the garden renovation. He seemed much more enthusiastic about the trip than I was, but at least there was the promise of lunch at my favorite restaurant, Trio. It had been several years since I ventured "up the hill" to the picturesque town at the foothills of the Blue Ridge Parkway made famous by its resident-turned-star, Andy Griffith. The locals claimed the old television show of the same name was based on Mount Airy, and busloads of tourists still flocked to Snappy Lunch to eat pork chop sandwiches, ride in a squad car replica like the one the Sheriff and his deputy used in the show, and see the collection of show memorabilia in one of two museums in the town. Tourists were looking for what no longer existed, a twilight zone of a friendly, welcoming hometown invented for the 1960s television show. Yet shop owners continued to oblige the fantasy by naming their diners character names and offering ice cream in old soda-fountain jerk outfits. T-shirt shops lined the street, and there were a few too many fiddler songs for my taste blaring from loudspeakers attempting to lure shoppers inside, but that was their story, and the downtown merchants were sticking to it.

The best lure for me, in addition to lunch at Trio, was definitely the antique shops. My favorite store was Sweet Apple Antiques, a place where I could find special treasures at reasonable prices. Soon, after a few conversations with Jack earlier in the week, a plan for a visit began to gel. Jack would have his conversation with the furniture maker, and I would tour antique stores and enjoy Trio and conversation with its owner, Chris Wishart, a long-time friend and sometimes confidant.

As I reached my driveway, Chairman Meow ran to greet me noisily. He had a neat collection of moles lined up in front of the door for me to inspect and purred loudly as I cooed over his hunting prowess. Though a neighbor had looked in on him while I was away, I knew this cat would never want for a tasty meal.

While the laundry machine did its thing, I sat on the screened porch with a glass of wine in one hand and Julia's garden plan/diary in the other. Using the commission's notes and plans from previous renovations, I was able to plan a reconstruction of several areas that had been destroyed by earlier efforts. The plan was shaping up nicely, though I had a few areas I wanted to revisit before I submitted my final plans for the commission's approval. Julia's diary—or plant journal, whatever it was—had been most helpful in answering a few questions, with its complete listing of plants, origins, and their locations in various spots around the garden. It also raised a few more questions I wasn't sure I needed to share with the commission at this time. Flipping through Julia's journal once more, my attention was held by a passage I must have missed in last week's late-night reading:

*I knew I shouldn't have done it, but I ventured to his cottage late last night. I was so taken by the way he talks so tenderly about the plants in the garden. And his eyes…his eyes are the bluest I've ever seen, so intense, like the brilliant blue of a delphinium in bloom. He had a pot of coffee on, but soon we were having wine. Since I haven't had much of it, I guess I got a little carried away. Well, more than a little. I needed to show him that I was the better choice, and that I cared far more for him than Mary ever could. I wanted him to kiss me, to take me in his strong arms, to touch me with his big, rough hands. I didn't think I could control my feelings any longer, but he stopped me from pushing him too far. He wants to date me, to court me properly, he said. I hated it that he was stronger and more in control of his feelings than I was, especially after all these years he's been dropping hints about his feelings, sitting close to me in the garden reading me poetry he'd written just for me, and the like. At that moment, my embarrassment turned to something I can't easily describe. He's been teasing and pursuing me for years, being all sweet and kind, and then when I finally decide…I decided…to give in, he turns me down! It makes me think that Mary is really his love interest, and his words just don't match his actions toward me. He continues to tease me, to string me along, but in truth, it must be Mary whom he loves!*

This "aha" moment was huge. Putting down my glass of wine, I read the passage several times. Julia had just become more fascinating—and considerably more dangerous. A woman scorned, after all, is not one to be toyed with, even by a longtime friend like her unnamed mystery man with the intense blue eyes.

Bingo! The mysterious Mister…. What was his name, the old man who came to visit me? Everett, Ebert, Evans. Yes, that was it. Mr. Evans. Would he know more? Quite probably. Either way, it was looking like it might be time for another visit to Columbia.

# Chapter Twelve

"Ready?" Jack popped his head inside my half-opened door, breaking my concentration on the grant documents in front of me. We hadn't spoken yet this week, what with client meetings and the usual work-load, so I was caught off guard in more ways than one by this interruption.

"Ready for what?"

"Our road trip to Mount Airy, remember? We talked about it last week? I spoke with the furniture maker this morning, and he said he's in today, but heading off to a show tomorrow. I want to go visit him before he goes so I can get my order in. Still interested in going with me?"

This may not have qualified as the kind of spontaneous adventure Ben had suggested I have, but it was the best I could manage at the moment. "Sure," I said as I closed my laptop and grabbed my purse. "Let's go."

Jack looked nearly as surprised as I felt. I was being spontaneous, and it felt kind of good. Our brief stop by the front desk to sign out for the day was met by raised eyebrows. Stephanie primed us for information as best she could.

"Client meeting or pleasure outing?"

"See you later, Steph." I shrugged my shoulders as we headed out the door. Hey, adventures were supposed to be mysterious, weren't they? "Coffee?"

"Definitely." Jack walked toward his Blazer, but I shook my head.

"Let's take my car. Then I know we'll make it home again in one piece."

"I'm deeply offended, Lily," Jack said, feigning a hurt look on his face. I wondered how fake it was, so I tossed him my car keys.

His mood bolstered, Jack drove us to Krankie's Coffee for cups of go-juice before navigating the downtown road construction between us and the highway. Jack seemed nearly joyful driving my Mini up the highway. Truthfully, I felt okay as a passenger, though his go-fast driving took a little getting used to for someone used to driving herself everywhere. I took the opportunity to call the restaurant to see about reservations, though I had hoped I wouldn't need them for today.

On our road trip, Jack shared his excitement about the furniture he planned to order today, and he repeated to me some of his conversation with the furniture maker about wood choices, special details of the dining table and chairs he was going to buy, what kind of fabric he was thinking about for the chairs, and the different array of options the furniture maker offered. Jack told me what he knew about the area where we were heading in relation to the furniture maker's shop, as well. After about twenty minutes, he seemed, thankfully, out of breath and out of steam on this topic.

By the time we reached the hilly stretch of road approaching Pilot Mountain, the patchwork landscape of farms and trees was getting to me. I was actually feeling relaxed.

Even from my vantage point in the passenger seat, I could see ravens circling the craggy face of the balding top of Pilot Mountain, a sturdy sentinel with a ravens' sanctuary on the mountaintop. "Years ago, people were allowed to climb the rock face up either a steep set of wooden stairs, or with personal climbing gear," Jack broke the silence. "I always wanted to do that, but they don't allow that anymore. Seems some poor soul died in a climbing accident, so the Park closed that option."

"I can see why," I said, craning my neck to see the top from my side of the car as we passed as closely as the highway allowed. "There is a walking path that runs around the base of that peak, if you ever wanted to get close to it without the danger. The trailhead begins at a parking lot near the top. My son and I have hiked several trails around Pilot Mountain, and that's one of our favorites."

"I've been there, too," Jack said. "When I first moved here, I hiked all over Pilot Mountain and Hanging Rock State Park. Both places are great. We should plan a day of hiking sometime. Do you like to camp?"

I hesitated before answering. Before Ben came along, Pete and I would sail to a national park, picnic, and camp on the beach. And when we first moved inland to Greensboro, we would take weekend trips to the mountains to explore places like Cade's Cove in the Great Smokey Mountains or various stops along the Blue Ridge Parkway. As I recalled, much of it was fun. Then Pete made *other* sleeping arrangements. "I used to, but it's been a long time."

"Well, it might be fun to do it again, and these parks are so close to Winston-Salem, if the weather turns bad, we can always pack it up and go home." Jack was positively buoyant at the idea.

"I'll think about it." I really did think it might be a good idea, even if I planned a camping trip without Jack. My noncommittal answer seemed sufficient for Jack. He didn't push the subject anymore.

A mix of mobile home parks and starter castles dotted the hills along our drive, an interesting juxtaposition between economic classes that some people refused to admit still existed. Poverty was very much a part of this county as evidenced by what little could be seen from the highway. Though parts of it looked postcard perfect, I knew it was a mirage. Our local paper often reported drug busts, meth labs, school bomb threats, etc. Sheriff Andy Taylor and his bumbling deputy would have had their hands full.

Though the distance from Winston-Salem to Mount Airy was roughly thirty-eight miles, this "Hollow," as it was known a century ago, settled in a ring of foothills, seemed to be a world away from home. The view to the valley opened up where the speed limit dropped and the highway ended. Mount Airy was tucked into tree-lined streets off to the right of the main road. The hazy Blue Ridge Mountains stretched out ahead of us. I sensed Jack's delight in his posture as he spoke about the mountains with fondness.

"When I hiked the Appalachian Trail, this stretch was a favorite of mine," he said, nodding at the purple-blue hills, which were coming more into focus the closer we got. "There are waterfalls and streams just off the trail, and the National Parks system maintains great campsites and shelters. It's been a while since I was up here. Have you ever been on the Blue Ridge Parkway?"

"A few times, on Girl Scout trips."

"Somehow, I just can't see you as a Girl Scout." Jack laughed a little.

"You're kidding, right? You saw what was in the trunk of my car. I'm always prepared."

"Good point. Only that's the Boy Scout motto."

"I was an early adopter of that saying. I hiked up here with our Scout troop a few times, and I've driven sections of the Parkway, as well. You're right—it's a lovely place. Where is your furniture maker's shop?"

"His directions say to go just a bit north of town. Here's what he sent me," Jack said, handing me a printed email with directions. "Oh, wait," Jack paused. "I just realized you may not want to wait on me while I talk to him about my order."

*Consideration runs high with this one,* I thought. "Honestly, I'd prefer you drop me off downtown. There's an antique store I want to visit, and then I want to go to Trio for lunch."

"Cool," Jack said as he made a quick turn into a small mall's parking lot. "I'll take you there, then buzz up to this guy's shop. I'll meet you at Trio for lunch in a bit. Will thirty minutes suit you for your antiquing?" Jack cruised down a side street that met a road we'd just passed, turned left toward downtown, and headed to Main Street.

"No rush," I answered. I'd forgotten about the possibility of him wanting to join me for lunch, but I should have considered it, given the time of day.

Jack turned right on the one-way Main Street, and at my direction, let me out in front of Sweet Apple Antiques. "Trio is on the back side of that green brick building just behind you," I offered.

"I'll find you," he replied as I got out of my own car. He waved and tootled off. It seemed weird, watching my car leave without me.

Wandering into the antique store, I heard the wooden floors creaking with my every step. That special smell of "old" ever-present in antique stores greeted me just as a fresh-faced woman seated behind a counter said hello. I could sense she was taking me in—appraising whether I was just looking or on a mission. Today, I just might be tempted.

Glass cabinets filled with collections of costume jewelry held my gaze for fifteen minutes. I felt a bit like a fish trying to decide between tempting fishing lures. One in particular captured my attention: shaped like a lily, a thin gold stem held curved petals of tiny purple and blue rhinestones set amid a mix of green and white "leaves" that sparkled in the glass case in front of me.

"If there's anything in the case you'd like to see, just let me know," the person behind the counter said cheerfully. Okay, she had me figured out. "The pieces in that cabinet are on sale. That's my cabinet, and I just decided."

"Your cabinet?"

"Yes, this antique store is staffed by the people who own the merchandise in each booth. We take turns manning the front desk here. So, if I say the items in that cabinet are on sale, they can be."

I liked this woman more and more. "Which is your favorite?"

"They all are, of course, and I've collected costume jewelry for years. That pin of the lily is quite lovely. Is that the one you'd like to see?"

"Sure," I said. "Why not?"

She opened the sliding glass door to the cabinet with a key kept behind the front counter. "This one is pretty. It would look really nice on that black top of yours." She pulled out the lily pin as well as two others for me to see. Beside the lily pin, she pulled out a bird with a small diamond-like rhinestone for an eye and a round brooch with a spiral of different colored rhinestones. The largest in the center was the color of a ruby. I loved all three instantly. "Could you keep these here at the counter? I'd like to look around a bit before I buy all three of them."

"Of course," she said with a triumphant smile. "Take all the time you want."

I looked at my watch. I didn't have all the time I wanted, but at least I could take a quick tour through the rest of the store. Jadeite plates and a mix of vintage cufflinks begged for a lingering look in one booth. A mix of vintage clothing, furniture, books, glass, and kitchenware in other neighboring booths gave my curious mind a workout, too. I reveled in the antique vase collection in one booth and chose a small glass bud vase to add to my own collection. Three rhinestone-studded pins and a bud vase later, I felt I had to leave in order to make my reservation at Trio. Besides, any more time spent in that antique store would have proved fatal to my budget. The salesperson was right: the lily pin looked stunning against my black shirt.

I strolled down the block leading away from the main street through the downtown section toward the back of a two-story brick building that had been painted a deep shade of green. The entrance to Trio Restaurant and Bar was to the back of the building. I climbed the stairs leading to the restaurant rather than taking an elevator.

"Hello, friend!" Chris Wishart called out to me as I reached the top steps and entered his restaurant. My old high school friend-turned-successful restaurateur hugged me and showed me to a table in the corner of the cozy dining room. One of several young servers brought water glasses and took a nod from Chris, which must have meant, *This is my special guest. Treat her well.* She departed, then quickly returned with a bottle of my favorite chardonnay without me even opening my mouth to place an order as if she had been primed on what to do when I arrived.

Chris knew how to treat his friends well here. "You've stayed away much too long, Kitty," he said, calling me by my high school nickname. "I've missed you're smiling face."

"And I've missed you, too." I meant it. Chris was one of my *gang of friends* back in the day. We were always together, our group, piling into cars for movies when we were younger, or hanging out at the mall in Winston-Salem. Chris, in particular, was my long-time confidant. He was there at my wedding, Ben's christening, and again by my side through my subsequent divorce. I attended his special events as well, including both of his young daughters' christenings. Over the years, we'd swapped plants and recipes, though I always thought I got the better end of the deal since he was a far better cook than I would ever be. And given the specials listed on the single-page, calligraphy-penned menu, today's lunch promised to be superb as well.

I filled Chris in on all that was happening at work and in my garden. We traded news of family and friends, and we laughed over an old joke or two until two other couples entered the restaurant and Chris excused himself to greet them fondly. After he'd helped them settle into their chairs, he waved to me and disappeared into the kitchen.

A gem among the other food offerings of Mount Airy, Trio sits on the top floor of an old brick warehouse-turned-shop-of-delights. Three floors filled with glassware, homewares, what-to-wears, and gifts seemed like a maze to the uninitiated. I recognized the dazed look on Jack's face when he wandered into Trio after what had probably been a too-long detour through shelves of gifts and gadgets. I waved and he made his way through the growing crowd of diners in the small restaurant. Wooden tables seating two to four guests a piece were filling fast, and a gentle hum of activity seemed to bounce off the brick walls encasing the small place. On the walls, I noted two of the larger brightly-colored paintings were of Chris' girls. They were as sweet on canvas as they were in person. I would have to visit them soon before they grew up and forgot who I was.

"I must have come in the wrong door," Jack said, finding his seat at the same instant our server appeared with an additional place setting and a glass for the chardonnay. Eyebrow raised, Jack looked at me. "Are we expecting a guest?"

"No, Chris—the owner—welcomed me with a quick visit before he headed back to the kitchen. He's a dear friend of mine. I hope he comes back out in a bit so you can meet him. He's also an awesome chef."

Jack's raised eyebrow remained arched. "Lily, is this fellow a friend or a *friend*?" I might have been mistaken, but for a second, I thought a flash of green passed across Jack's face. Was he jealous?

"A dear friend from high school, Jack. We used to run with a large circle of friends, doing everything together."

"Sounds like a pack of wolves, if you ask me."

Ignoring his attempt at humor, I trudged on and poured him a glass of wine. "How was your visit with the furniture maker?"

"His shop is amazing," effused Jack. He took a sip of wine and smiled. "It's about four-thousand square feet of woodworking equipment and lumber. He has every kind of wood imaginable, and he showed me wood samples, plus a few designs of the pieces I'm interested in that he was modifying for clients. He told me about his process, from the initial drawings on paper to the finished product, and he even shared his fabric swatches with me. He really has his act together. It's amazing that he can do what he does there by himself."

"Did you pull the trigger and place an order?"

"I couldn't resist. I ordered a dining table and chairs, a buffet cabinet that looks sort of like a shoji screen on the front, and a tall tower lamp. They are going to look awesome." Jack clearly was pleased with his purchases. He pulled out his phone and showed me the furniture maker's website so I could see for myself the types of items he purchased. "These are a little different than what he's making for me, but you get the general idea." The pictures were spectacular, with incredible attention given to every detail in each piece.

"How long will it take for him to build all of that?"

"That's a bit of an unknown, but perhaps sometime in the fall. It would be great to get it before Thanksgiving, but since he makes it by himself, it may take a while to complete it all. He has lots of other orders to fill and shows to do between now and then. He said he might be able to get it done before the Piedmont Craftsmen's Fair in November. Have you been to that before?" Jack didn't wait for me to answer, though I had been to the show many times. "It's a fantastic venue for artists of all kinds. They set up in the Convention Center in Winston-Salem, and it's a real treat for anyone with an eye toward art. I first met this furniture maker at a similar show in Asheville a few years ago. I know it will be a while before I get the furniture, but it will be worth the wait." Catching his breath for a second, Jack changed the subject. He leaned forward and softened his tone. "Hey, we need to make a toast." His face looked serious.

I raised my glass, not sure what to expect.

"Here's to solving the mystery of what happened in Julia's garden."

"Beg pardon?" I was astounded.

"I've been thinking about that journal or diary or whatever you call it. I've been reviewing the newspaper clippings again, too. For the longest time, I was thinking it was more like a plant journal, but some of the passages made me wonder."

"Go on."

"According to early entries in Julia's journal, the poor kid was clearly a party girl. Then something drastic happened. I did a little more digging in the library, and I decided to call an old buddy of mine to see if he could help me out."

"When did you do this?" Jack was full of surprises.

"Last week. He shot me an email this morning before we left that might be interesting," Jack said, pulling a folded piece of paper from his plaid shirt pocket. "It's a copy of an old newspaper clipping he dug up in the state archives. It's a great little place for research, by the way. I thought it would be better to share this with you when we were away from the office." He handed me the paper and took a sip of wine.

In that instant, Chris came back to our table for introductions and to take our order personally. The bread he brought was warm. "Chris, this is Jack Chapman, a coworker and…a friend of mine." I felt I should clarify our relationship for both men present. "Jack is a civil engineer."

"Glad to meet you, Jack," Chris said as he shook Jack's hand. "Lily and I go way back to high school days. She's one of the truest friends you'll ever meet. So what brings you to Mount Airy today?"

"Furniture. I met with an artist who has his shop here. Gorgeous stuff. We were just talking about the craft fairs where he shows his work, and that's how I met him. It's amazing that he lives here, not too far from Winston-Salem. He's incredibly talented, and his work is carried in galleries all over the place."

"Does he sell his work through the High Point furniture showrooms?" Chris asked.

"No, just through the craft shows and his website. Here's his card." Jack handed the furniture maker's card to Chris. Then he handed Chris his phone to share pictures of the website he had only moments earlier shared with me. "You might want to check it out sometime. Have you met him?"

"Oh, yes, he comes in from time to time with his family. Nice guy," Chris said. "And that's fantastic you've come to see him today—it's been a while since Lily and I have visited."

"Too long," I chimed in.

"You'll have to come more often. I have a few new recipes to share. Why don't you two come up to the farm for lunch one Sunday? I know my girls would love to see their Aunt Kitty."

Jack looked questioningly at me. "Aunt Kitty?"

"I'll tell you about it later," I said, heading him off. "That sounds like an invitation too good to pass up. For today, though, Chris, what would you recommend?"

• • •

I knew I was in love with the crab cake dish as soon as the server set it in front of me. It looked as good as it smelled.

Jack took a bite of his dish of shrimp risotto served with leeks, tomatoes, and spinach. "Wow!" It was all he could manage as he plowed through his meal.

Before I lifted my fork to the tempting dish in front of me, I quickly scanned the article Jack had offered me before our lunch arrived. It was a gossip column from the local tattler, where socialites were mentioned and their lovely evening gowns described in great detail. No detail was too small, so the article also included lists of hairstyles and corsages of orchids adorning each belle's gown. The descriptions were elegant, but it was the circled item in the last column inch that made my palms sweat. "Jack, we have to go to Columbia."

"I was hoping you'd say that. I've been itching for a road trip." Jack took a triumphant last bite of his lunch. "I think this calls for dessert."

I ate my crab cake while he placed an order for chocolate ganache torte and coffee for each of us. I was going to need every bit of caffeine I could get my hands on for the three-hour drive after this wine-infused lunch. Luckily, my adrenaline rush was starting to kick in: Julia's garden, here we come.

# Chapter Thirteen

"So, *Aunt Kitty*, do you feel like driving, or shall I?" Jack's smugness was palpable as we rose from our seats to leave. Chris dashed out of the kitchen for a hug and an admonishment not to be a stranger.

"Let's stay in touch better, Lily," he said. "I mean it about the two of you coming up to the farm for the day. The girls would love to see you again. You'll probably not recognize how much they've grown since your last visit."

Ignoring his comment that placed Jack and me in the "Two of Us" category, I plunged ahead. "I promise, Chris, I'll come soon. I'll call you next week when I have my calendar open in front of me, and we'll set a date for it. That will give me a chance to figure out which plants I'll bring in exchange for the wonderful meal I know you'll create for me." I hugged him. "See you soon, friend!"

Jack and Chris shook hands again, and we headed out the door and down the stairs to a large parking lot behind the building.

"I'll drive," I said, taking the car keys Jack dangled in front of me as we walked to the car. "You should probably call the office to let Stephanie know we won't be back today."

"Oh, I can hear the scandalous talk, now," Jack smiled. "The rumors will be flying around that place like Nerf bullets in the late afternoon showdown."

A smile crept over my lips. Adventures sometimes involved a little scandal, so this seemed like a great one to begin. "Let them talk."

"Why, Lily! I'm shocked," Jack feigned surprise. "What about my reputation?"

"Don't worry; it will be intact when we return to the office. I promise."

While Jack called the office and explained that we were called away to Columbia for an unexpected meeting, I pointed the car toward Columbia. If we were lucky, we'd miss the traffic jam that surrounds Charlotte most every afternoon.

Jack persisted. "Tell me about this name Kitty."

"It was just a high school nickname. We all had them back in the day. I was called Kitty because I like cats. Nothing scandalous there."

"And what was Chris's nickname?"

"Red, or sometimes Carrot Top, on account of his red hair. Some of our friends had multiple names, but I was just 'Kitty.' It's simple, really, and it was quite harmless. I knew I was part of the 'in' crowd when I was given a nickname."

"It suits you." Jack's look suggested he was sincere.

"I've always treasured it, just as I treasure my friendship with Chris. Not many of us in that gang have stayed in contact over the years, but our friendship has lasted through a lot of...stuff." I didn't want to elaborate on what that *stuff* was. To my great relief, Jack didn't ask.

He did, however, ask the obvious. "Did you two date?"

I hesitated in answering. "I'm not sure what constituted dating because we hung out with a large group of friends. A few of these friends ended up as couples, but most of us did stuff together as a group. Chris was one of my 'go-with' friends."

"A go-with friend? This is sounding serious, like a going-steady friend might be," Jack said.

"No, it wasn't like that. When I needed someone to go with me to an event or an attraction like a museum or to hear the symphony that none of my other friends wanted to go see, Chris always volunteered. I did the same for him. I was his go-with friend. Even from an early age, we enjoyed the plays and musical events held at the School of the Arts. Not too many of our friends were into that at the time. Our parents are good friends and neighbors, so we hung out a lot on the weekends when our friends might have been doing other things. Since both of our families enjoyed the art offerings at the School of the Arts, well, we often went together, even when we got older. When Chris got his driver's license, it was one of the first things we did: we took in a show together, without our parents in tow."

"Oh, so a go-with is a friend with no fringe benefits."

I smiled at the thoughts I wouldn't share. "A go-with is a friend, pure and simple."

"I get it."

"Have you ever had a go-with friend, Jack?"

"Not until now. That's what we are, isn't it?"

"Yes, I guess that's what we are: go-with friends."

I wasn't sure I heard correctly, but I thought I heard Jack mutter something that sounded like, "Well, it's a start." We'd see if it was.

• • •

It was late in the afternoon by the time we reached Columbia. The properties of the historic district were still open, and a few visitors milled about, snapping pictures of the stately homes guarded by centuries-old oak trees lining the streets. Given that it was the middle of the week, two groups of students were in the garden. One group was clearly engaged with an animated docent who shared the history of a large brick mansion across from the Norton-Grace property. A second group of rambunctious children stood in what might have been called a line, preparing to board a yellow school bus. A feeling of hope washed over me as I thought of the garden restoration work to be done on the Norton-Grace Mansion: maybe after we were done, the transformation of the property's grounds would help bring the same kind of joy and wonder to future groups of visiting schoolchildren.

I parked my car at the end of the street. As we walked along the edge of the property, I peered in through the wrought-iron gates that topped the low wall. This structure had changed over the years, and while the bars of the wrought iron fence and gate might not have been historically accurate, the open expanse of the garden leading up to the grand home could be seen from the street, enticing visitors the way a solid wall might not have done. I, for one, was willing to let that inaccuracy slide.

Jack and I prepared to show our credentials as we entered the gated property, but there didn't seem to be anyone around. "Where is everyone?" Jack pondered. "There are still tons of people across the street. It's kind of eerie being the only ones here."

"Maybe it was an earlier stop on their tour of properties," I said, scanning the grounds. "And I don't think we're alone." I pointed to the garden's last remaining greenhouse just as a figure moved slowly across the doorway. Instinctively, we picked up our pace as we headed to the greenhouse.

"Hello?" I called out, not sure whom I might be speaking to. "Anyone here?"

A gruff voice responded from a dim corner of the building. "Tours are done for the day; you'll have to come back tomorrow."

"We're not here for a tour," Jack spoke first. "We came to speak to you. It's Mr. Evans, right?"

Stepping partially out from his hiding place, the tall man who came to visit me in my office with an offering of Julia's diary looked alarmed. "You know my name?"

"It's okay; he's with me," I called. "I'm Lily McGuire, and you brought me a journal—Julia's journal; remember? We just wanted to talk for a few minutes."

"I remember who you are," he said cautiously. "What did you want to talk about?"

"Julia."

With that, he stepped forward so I could see him fully. "Did you find it?"

"I'm not exactly sure what I'm looking for. Perhaps you could tell me."

"You still don't know, do you?" Mr. Evans snorted. "I thought for sure you could figure it out. Well, if you're not here to help, you had better leave. I'm about to close the place up for the day."

I stood firm. "We'll leave in just a minute, but first, I need you to tell me about your relationship with Julia." Judging by the color draining quickly from his otherwise ruddy cheeks, I could guess what kind of relationship they'd had. His now pale face made me worry that he might pass out at any moment. Jack must have thought the same thing, too.

Jack pointed to a low gardening bench. "Why don't we all sit down? You can tell us what happened." Jack and I moved slowly toward Mr. Evans as if he were an apparition about to vanish.

Mr. Evans sank onto the bench and breathed deeply. "I'll tell you. I knew this day would come. First of all, my name is Evans. Not Mr. Evans as you presumed, but Evans Merritt. I've been tending to these gardens for decades."

"Were you in love with Julia?" The words tumbled out of my mouth before I could stop them.

"Yes," he said, sighing. It seemed as though a tremendous burden had just been lifted from his sagging shoulders, and he looked two inches taller that instant. "I loved her beyond reason. I was here when Julia's family bought the property. From the first day I saw her, I knew I was in love. She was a few years younger than me, but I knew in that instant, we would always be together." Evans seemed lost in thought for a few minutes.

"Tell us about her," I encouraged him.

"She often brought new plants to the garden that she found in different places. Some were gifts from friends. Others, well, let's just say she was good at foraging and liberating plants. She didn't right much care where they came from, truth be told. Julia had a vision of what they should look like that I never quite understood. I did whatever she asked, and was happy for it. I wrote poetry back in the day, and sometimes, she'd sit real close to me to speak because I don't hear so well. I guess you could say I was more comfortable around plants and Julia than other people on account of my hearing loss. She never seemed to mind it, though. Anyway, I shared much of my poetry with her, and she seemed to enjoy our time together when no one else was around to see. Since I read her journal, though, I realize how she really felt—like she wanted to be with me, but I was the hired help, and, well, that wasn't proper back then. A fellow had to come from the right family to be in a circle with a woman like Julia.

I didn't, see. And unfortunately, Julia always had a sense of what was proper. Me, well, I just followed my heart."

Things were starting to make sense. Evans must be the mystery man in Julia's diary. I softly approached the subject of what happened to Julia as best I could. "Evans, in her diary, Julia's tone changed from carefree to somewhat dark and disturbing. Can you tell us what happened to her?"

His brow furrowed for a second, as if he were thinking...remembering. "When she was younger, Julia was always the life of the party. She was by far the loveliest creature in town, and everybody who met her was instantly infatuated with her. She was charming, so full of life, and gracious. She treated everyone she met to a beautiful smile, so it was hard for me not to fall under her spell, too. The difference for me was that my love was genuine...not the sort of game some of the young suitors played, mind you. They just wanted to flirt and carry on with her. I told her what I thought of a few of them boys, too. Secretly, I wanted to marry Julia, but I didn't see no way that it would work out. I could barely approach her papa, you know, look him in the eye, and tell him how I felt. He was a huge man, both physically and in his standing in this community. There's no way he would have ever said I could court her, not with my background and all. Looking back on it, I think she was amused by my jealousy of the other fellows. I guess she was eager for company because when no one else was around, she'd spend hours at my side, here in this very greenhouse, repotting seedlings, tending to orchids, listening to my poetry. I started writing more and more of it for her to let her know how I felt about her.

"I thought I would capture her heart with my sincerity, and that we would figure out the rest as we went along. I didn't have a lot of money back then—well, not many of us did. That became a focus of mine: if I were to court her, I'd want to do it properly. I started working a second job at night over at the military base. I didn't get called up to serve on account of my hearing loss, so this was the small thing I felt I could do for the war effort, even though the war was about to be over by that time. I did whatever I could to start building a nest egg. I figured she'd know what I was up to since I left for work the second I got off of my job here in the gardens, but I guess I was wrong."

"What do you mean?"

"She came to see me one evening. At first, she accused me of seeing some other woman in town. Well, she figured I had to be, since I ran off every afternoon after my work here was done. I was surprised at how she spoke to me, because until that minute, I didn't think I was making any headway in showing her I was worthy. She just never told me how she felt about me. Of course, I told her none of that was true, and that I was busy with something else that needed to be done for a specific purpose. After she calmed down a bit, we chatted about gardening, about life, about our dreams. I offered her a glass of wine—I wasn't even thinking about trying to take advantage of her, but I guess she had too much to drink and wanted to kiss and the like. I told her I'd rather wait until I could court her properly before we got all hot and bothered the way she clearly wanted to that night, and she got real mad. I didn't know what to make of it. I told her to go home, as that was the honorable thing to say, though I tell you now, I really wanted her to stay. I sometimes wondered what would have happened if she had stayed that night."

"So she left with her…" Jack searched for the right word, "her dignity?"

"Yep," Evans said. "I thought she'd feel better about things in the morning that way. The next day, though, she seemed a little colder to me. For the life of me, I will never understand women. Uh, no offense, Miss McGuire."

"None taken," I said with a smile. Now I understood totally what had happened between Julia and him, even if he didn't. "What happened next?"

"Like I said, I worked really hard. I took the other job purposely so I could save up enough money to buy her a promise gift to show my intentions. It was a magnificent brooch I had the jeweler design with opals set in a flurry of small diamonds. It looked like a flower blossoming, and I felt certain it would be perfect for her, and the deeper-colored opals reminded me of the color of Julia's eyes. The brooch was about two-and-a-half inches long, and nearly as wide. There were several other choices I could have made, but this particular brooch was just what I wanted. It seemed so organic, the way the gold and platinum flower stalks were arranged. Plus, it was what I could afford, and I felt sure it would be the best way for me to show Julia that I was more than just the help: I was worthy of her love and affection. Why, the day I gave it to her, she was so happy! I'll never forget that look of joy on her beautiful face. She looked at me with such tenderness that day, and I knew she felt the same way about me. I just knew it. She hugged me and thanked me for it, then said she wanted to show it off to her friends. I was certain we'd just turned a corner in our relationship. I felt a proper courting could begin. I gathered my courage to ask her papa if I could call on her, and I made a plan for every roadblock that he might throw in my face. I was ready for him, and I was ready for Julia to tell her friends what I really meant to her. So, at the next big party of the Christmas holiday season that was to see some more of the boys off to war, I showed up in the best suit I could borrow. I thought she'd be so pleased to have me at her side, but what she did sent us all into a tailspin."

Evans seemed agitated at the memory of what came next. To calm him, I offered him a half-drunk water bottle that was sitting on the workbench. After he'd had a few sips, he seemed calmer. I asked him to continue.

"I'll never forget that day," he started, his voice shaky. "It was a huge party at one of her friends' homes. I caught a ride to the party with the members of the band, who were all swell guys. They were nice to me, and all. I had even arranged for them to play one of Julia's favorite tunes by Glen Miller. They were going to announce a special dance, and I was going to take her hand and escort her to the middle of the wooden platform that had been set up especially for dancing in the middle of this garden. I just knew this was the beginning of many parties together. I wouldn't be an outsider anymore, with her at my side. Anyway, she was wearing the brooch, and it looked perfect. *She* looked perfect. Her dress was lavender, and she wore her long brown hair in a style I hadn't seen her wear before. She looked…elegant. She looked mature, too—like a woman, not the skinny girl who had dug in the garden with me all the years before. If there were ever a doubt about us being together, it evaporated in a second when she extended her hand to me in greeting." Evans shook his head and snorted. "What a fool I was to think she could really care for me. I read her journal over and over for a clue, some hint that she really did want to be in my life the same way I wanted her to be."

"Evans, what happened to change all that?" Jack jumped in. Like me, I guessed he was mesmerized by the story.

"Julia led me to a table where there were snacks and drinks. It was three steps from the dance floor, so I figured we'd have a drink while the band set up their equipment, then dance to show everyone we were officially a couple. I was so proud, so in love. Her friend Mary was there, too. Julia reached over to hand me a drink and then gave one to Mary that she said she'd made just for her. She called it a special recipe. I remember being thrilled to know that Mary and Julia could be so close, because I was sure Mary had told Julia how much I cared for her. I had shown Mary the brooch intended for Julia a few days before, and Mary said she was sure it would be what any girl would want. I thought certainly this would be the beginning of being accepted into their circle of friends, you know? Before Mary could take the drink from Julia, though, this other fellow, a suitor of Julia's, came up to the table. He slapped me on the back good-naturedly, and asked Julia to dance the first dance that the band was striking up at that moment. She looked flustered, and I took that as a sign that she wanted to be with me.

"I said as much, you know? This other fellow, though, he was persistent. Mary offered him her drink as a way to distract him from Julia, I think. Of course, he guzzled it right down and grabbed Julia's hand. He pulled her toward the dance floor just as the music started to play. Then he doubled over, clutched at his stomach, and fell to the ground. Julia shrieked, and then everything was just a blur. She ran from the party as a crowd was gathering around that poor fellow. Somebody was screaming for a doctor. I ran after Julia, and I caught up with her just as she was getting in her car. I jumped in as she was about to drive away. I tried to tell her not to run, not to be scared, but she just kept pounding on the steering wheel of her car and yelling, "It wasn't supposed to be this way!" I can still hear her. It's like an echo that's never gone from my head. I quickly put two and two together. She meant that drink for Mary. I don't know what was in it, but I saw the results when that boy hit the floor.

"The sad thing about it? I didn't care. I forgave her instantly, you know, because I realized at that second that she must have loved me enough to fight for me. She thought Mary and I were.... Well, she was unnecessarily jealous of us. I asked her to pull over so I could drive. I think she was exhausted, so she let me. As I drove, I started to think up a plan. She didn't seem to have any energy to fight me on it, so I took over."

"We read the newspaper clippings about the ransom note and the money, Evans." Jack spoke what was on my mind. "That was your plan?"

"I figured if I had money, she'd finally agree to marry me. I figured we'd elope, or just skip town. She was afraid she'd have to go to jail for killing that fellow, and I was bound and determined to protect her, no matter what it took."

"But you didn't tell her the truth, did you?" Jack's voice was calm, but I noticed the veins on his temple were trembling.

"How could I tell her? Once we had ditched her car, and then I got her papa's money, there was no turning back. I wanted to protect her. It would have been considered attempted murder, the poison in the drink."

"Not if nobody found out. Many toxic plants cause reactions that can be mistaken for other illnesses," I offered.

"Doesn't matter," Evans said. Tears were streaming down his face. "Julia was scared. I drove her back toward the house and snuck her in the servants' entrance out back. She took time only to pack a small bag. I did the same at my cottage, wary of seeing anyone. There wasn't anyone here because her parents were still out at another Christmas party, and I guess they hadn't heard what happened to the fellow at our party. Julia and I had agreed to meet at her car, but when I looked for her, she wasn't there. I searched the grounds, and finally found her here in the greenhouse. She wasn't wearing the brooch. That nearly broke my heart. She said she had put it in a safe place, and that once she was far enough away from Columbia, I could go back to get it for her. At that moment, I thought I would sail over the moon. She wanted us to be together. Right then and there, I pledged to do whatever it took to keep her safe from harm."

"Honorable," Jack said as he crossed his arms over his chest, "but not entirely honest." He reached into his shirt pocket and pulled out the article he'd shared earlier with me at lunch. He thrust it at Evans, who glanced at it for only a second. Clearly, he'd seen it before.

"I couldn't tell her," Evans protested, "not after she hinted we'd be together! If I had told her that fellow had just been diagnosed with a bad stomach bug and that he only spent a day throwing up in the hospital, why, she'd have raced back to his side and begged forgiveness from her parents. She probably would have done the same with Mary, who would never know the drink was really laced with something bad intended for her. If I had told Julia that her concoction only resulted in a stomach ache for that fellow, then I'd be out of a job, and out of her life for good! I decided it would be best to keep it a secret. Besides, I didn't get a chance to tell her until many years later. She certainly didn't know what had happened to him when we were in the greenhouse that day before she disappeared."

"This has been haunting you for years, hasn't it, Evans?" I spoke tenderly as I watched his shoulders sag again.

"You have no idea how hard it's been. No one knows this but you two."

"Your secret is safe," I said, putting my hand on his arm.

"Too bad it didn't work out the way you thought it would, though." Jack sounded irritated. "You messed up her life, you know, by not encouraging her to stick around and face the music for her actions."

"It wasn't just her life I messed with. It was mine, too. We went through with my plan, you see. We abandoned her car just outside of town, over near the military base. There wasn't much traffic on the dirt road we took, so nobody saw us leave it there. Then I got her a hotel room—it was the best I could afford. I told her I'd take care of everything, then come back for her in two days' time. All she had to do was wait for me. I walked back to Columbia, wrote the ransom note, and then clocked her papa over the head when he delivered the money to the park like I'd asked him to. It was a simple plan. And it worked." Evans took a deep breath, and added, "almost."

"Let me guess," Jack said. "When you got back to the hotel room where you'd left Julia, she wasn't there."

Evans nodded his head.

"And you kept the money for yourself?"

"I didn't know what else to do! I left my position at the estate and searched everywhere for Julia. I got an apartment in town, too, just in case she came back. I never stopped looking for Julia—or loving her."

"You do realize her parents probably lost their minds over her disappearance."

"I know, and I will never forgive myself for letting them suffer like that. I hoped I would be able to find her, to bring her home again. I wanted to make it right for her, for me, for her parents. For everybody, really. But I wasn't able to find her. Nobody could. Her parents hired a detective. He grilled everyone at that party, including me, but he didn't have any more luck than I did in finding her. Soon after that, her family sold the property and moved to the coast. I never heard anything more about them."

"How did you end up back here, in this job again?" I tried to be patient as he took a long drink of water.

"After Julia's family sold the property, I approached the new owners about getting my old job back. The more I thought about the timing of things that happened that day of the party, I felt sure Julia would have had only enough time to hide her brooch in the greenhouse or in the garden when we came back to get a few clothes. It was a stroke of luck that I found her journal in this very greenhouse among the gardening books I used to keep on the shelf, just there, in the corner." He nodded to a small corner cabinet in great need of a paint job. "The new owners weren't big on gardening, but they were big on appearances, so they hired me. I even got my old quarters back. While it may have appeared to them that I was just tending to the gardens, I was searching everywhere I could to find that brooch. I have yet to find it."

"And you're convinced it's in the garden? Are you sure it wasn't in Julia's things when she left?" Jack was being less than tactful. "Maybe she pawned it for cash."

"I thought that might be the case at first, too. In her journal, she even said she'd put it in a safe place in the garden," Evans said.

I must have missed that page of the diary. "Did she say that in the last two pages?"

"She did, but when I looked again for her statements about hiding the brooch in the garden, I didn't find them because the pages had been torn out. I swear, I remember reading them soon after I found her journal in the greenhouse, but they were missing when I brought the journal to you.

"I searched through the greenhouse for other clues she might have left, of course, but I was convinced she left it here in the garden for me to find and to bring to her when the time was right. I waited years for her to contact me to tell me where to search, but that didn't happen. When your boss lady first showed an interest in the garden, I got nervous. I felt sure she'd find it."

"What are you talking about?" Jack clearly was losing whatever patience he had left.

"I watched her—and you, Miss McGuire—walk through the gardens, making your plans and asking all kinds of questions. I was concerned that she would find the brooch—the brooch that I intended for Julia to have as a promise of my love. I figured it might be uncovered during the renovation that I knew was in the works. Before you came back with what I assumed would be your backhoes, I took Julia's diary and searched the grounds one last time. Things just didn't look the same, though, with many of the original plants gone or so overgrown; they didn't look the same as they did when Julia and I planted them."

"So you were trying to find it before Macy did?"

"Macy?" Evans looked confused. "The boss lady, yes, Macy. A few months later, Macy came upon me in the garden as I was working. I didn't hear her at first as I'm a little hard of hearing. When I realized she was speaking to me, I gave her a short tour of the garden. Then I returned to my greenhouse. About an hour later, she surprised me when she came in and stood beside me at my workbench. I didn't have a chance to put away Julia's journal, and she asked me what I had. I showed her the diary. As she combed through it, she lit up like a Christmas tree, noting the treasure of lists on the pages unlike what she'd seen available to her before through the historical plant surveys. She wanted to keep the diary, but I told her no, it was mine, and I wasn't going to share it. I felt I deserved to keep this last piece of Julia with me. Macy was kind about it. She said she'd make copies of it and return it to me. At first, I was firm about this, but in the greenhouse, she was so pleasant, so open. I trusted her, so I gave her the journal with hopes that she'd help me sort things out. I watched her put it into her giant bag she wore on her shoulder, and then I started to wonder if I would never see it again."

"But she didn't get a chance to read any of its pages, did she?" I was mentally checking off a calendar in my head, recounting our site visits. That was a year ago. Macy knew about the journal before she died of an apparent heart attack. "You know she had a heart attack, right?"

"That's the thing, see. She didn't have a heart attack; well, not in the traditional sense," Evans shook his head vigorously. "I had collected samples of all the plants listed in Julia's notes and kept them alive in this very greenhouse. These were the plants that Julia had brought from the beach, I suppose. I helped her plant each one in a section of the garden that she was partial to—she called it her secret garden spot. Using that journal, I had collected and cataloged the toxic ones, too. I had them all lined up here, on the workbench. When she walked into the greenhouse, Macy must have recognized several of them immediately as oddities to the garden. She touched several of them in a row without using gloves. For some people, the toxicity is nothing more than contact dermatitis. For Macy, though, the results of touching that many of them at one time were fatal," assured Evans. "The result was a paralysis that set in quickly. Before I could call for help, her heart stopped. I reclaimed the journal from her big bag and hid it before calling for help. I was so scared, but I felt that if I went to prison for her death, at least there would be some justice for everything else I'd done in my past."

# Chapter Fourteen

I didn't know what to make of Evans' story. "You've been searching a long time for that brooch," I said slowly. "Why on earth would you bring Julia's journal to me, after all these years? Were you giving up on the brooch?"

"Far from it, Miss McGuire. A few months ago, you came for another visit to the garden. It's been neglected so long, and I can scarcely keep up with it at this point. You'd never know that many, many years ago, it was one of the most talked about gardens in this state. Articles featuring this place regularly appeared in newspapers and magazines, and visitors from all over came to visit. It truly was something to behold. Anyway, that day I saw you in the garden, you reminded me of the way Julia used to look. Something about you made me feel like I could trust you with Julia's special diary. I've searched the grounds for years without finding what I wanted. I am running out of time, you see. The journal is of no use to me, so I thought you might be able to figure out where she hid it in the gardens. All I want, Miss McGuire, is that brooch. I spent everything I had on it once, and since then, I've spent about everything I have trying to keep the other thing I treasure close to me.

"Julia?"

Evans nodded, his tears flowing freely now. "Yes, Julia. I found her some years ago, long after the house had been sold out of the family. She was broken in spirit, and in pocket. Back then, she said she'd been surviving on wages from whatever meager job she could find. She said she had somehow managed to find a ride to the beach the day after the party where she found work in a small gift shop that first summer, making just enough to feed herself and to pay for a room in a boarding house. When the season was over, the owners of the store had pity for her and sent her to stay with their relatives in Florida where she worked as a waitress for years. That's where I found her. I traveled everywhere I thought she might have gone, showing a small photo I had of her to anyone who would take time to listen. I finally found her in that restaurant, though she worked more as a hostess by then. The light in her eyes told me immediately that she recognized me, and I asked her to come home. At first, she wasn't sure she could. She said she worried that if she had come back to Columbia sooner, she would have been found guilty of murdering the suitor. I tried to tell her that he didn't die that day, but she didn't believe me. She said she thought I was trying to comfort her, to make her feel better about the way things happened. She just kept repeating the same story, over and over. Her mind, is, well, now she has dementia. I felt sorry for her, sure, but I still brought her home where I could care for her, like an old friend would. I've been taking care of her all these years."

"What did the property owners think of all this?" I asked, engrossed in Evans' tale.

"The new owners of the house didn't seem to notice her, and they didn't bother us. Last year, when this mansion and grounds became the property of the historical preservation group, I moved her to a small two-bedroom apartment in town. The preservation folks said I could stay on in my little cottage to help take care of the place as best I could, and to act as a tour guide. I've been grateful for their generosity. I kept asking Julia to help me find the brooch, or at least to help me decipher her notes in the journal. Unfortunately, Julia couldn't help me. With her dementia, none of it made sense to her anymore. She continually recounted the parties, the dresses, the days gone by, and…the accident. She got to the point where I couldn't take care of her anymore by myself. Had to move her to a special assisted living place that specializes in cases like hers. I didn't tell them who she really was, and you know, they didn't seem to care, either. I want to find the brooch before it's too late. You see, I need to find it now more than ever. My time here is running out."

My heart went out to him in that instant. "I'll see what I can do to find it."

"Thank you." Evans stood up and shook my hand.

"Evans?" It was Simon calling from the doorway of the greenhouse. "Are you bothering this nice lady?" He walked a few steps into the greenhouse and faced me as if I were the only one there. "And how are you, my dear? You look as ravishing as ever. I didn't expect to see you here. Or is there a meeting that I didn't know about?" He turned a steely gaze first on Evans, then on Jack. "Perhaps with this man?" He pointed to Evans.

"No, no meeting," I offered casually. "Jack and I are in town to visit a few of the other properties and to see if the remaining structures on the property are still viable enough to include in the restoration. This nice gentleman was telling me about the history of the greenhouse, plus the other structures that used to be on the property. It must have been an extremely productive garden in its day, with him in charge."

Simon looked askance at me. "Yes, and as I am sure you noted on the plans, this was but one of several greenhouses. If you would like, I can tour you through the house today. It's closed to visitors, now, but I have a key to the mansion. Besides, it's probably been a while since you've seen the interior, and we've covered so much ground since our initial meetings." Simon tugged at my arm, leading me toward the mansion and on a tour I wasn't the least interested in taking.

Jack nodded for me to go ahead. "I'll be along in a minute. I just wanted to get a few more measurements to confirm what we're planning in the garden."

I caught his drift, and I felt certain Evans did, too.

As Simon bored me with his account of the many times the mansion had been renovated or had changed owners, I tried to imagine what it had looked like when Julia was living there. At this point, the two-storied Federal-style mansion with its white Doric columns and gracious porch was painted a tasteful, if not demure, color of beige with off-white trim on its many windows and fascia boards. Symmetrical in design, matching doors on each level were painted a pale shade of green, the top door opening to a deck with a commanding view. Stone arches accentuated with keystones topped each door and window on both floors. On what I presumed was the attic floor was an arched fan-shaped window centered over the doors. Topped by two chimneys, the house was, at least from my view of it, well-appointed.

Since my focus had always been the gardens, I hadn't paid too much attention to the house on my tour of the property with Macy. Now that I had an understanding of Julia's world, I could see how important a role the house had in shaping who she was and perhaps why she may have thought what she did about hired help, like Evans.

By today's standards, this place was the equivalent of a decent-sized home, but it wouldn't rival many of the McMansions seen everywhere. When it was built in the late 1700s, it would have been considered a grand estate. It was a shame that much of the eight acres of land once surrounding the property had been sold off over the years.

I wished Jack would hurry so he could come rescue me from Simon before we entered the mansion. I feared for my sanity if I had to listen to him drone on too much longer about what grand plans he had for the house. Simon caught my gaze back toward the greenhouse. "Am I to wait on Jack, or shall we go on ahead?"

"I was just wondering about the caretaker, or gardener. He seemed so knowledgeable about the gardens that I was hoping to speak with him before he leaves for the day."

"Oh, he won't leave. Seems like he'll never leave, even though the commission said it was time for him to go at the end of the year. Evans has been here so long that I'm beginning to think he was born in one of those greenhouses," Simon said dryly. "He really must think about retiring soon. I think he's going to scare our guests one of these days."

End of the year? That's what Evans meant when he said he was running out of time. "How long have you known him?" I asked as calmly as I could, though I felt like hitting Simon with something heavy as we walked through a restored arbor. Blossoms of wisteria were peeking out from behind brightly-colored leaves. Fortunately for Simon, I didn't spot any heavy objects worthy of hurling at him.

"Evans? Oh, he was here when I first started on the project." Simon wasn't interested in filling in the backstory, other than to let me know he didn't much care for the man. "He has been a caretaker or gardener or something like that on this property for about a million years."

"I noted a caretaker's cottage on the plans. Is that his?"

"It is. It's around that hedge of boxwoods, out of sight from the main house. We were able to stop an overzealous renovation team—the one before I joined the project—from getting carried away with their efforts. They wanted to knock it down. We weren't so fortunate to stop them from tearing up a few of the other structures. As I'm sure you're aware, this property has a star-studded past. It has served as many different entities, including a college. At its zenith of history, it had stables and servants' quarters, an outside kitchen, a summer house, and more greenhouses than what was able to be saved. That one you were in today is probably the newer of the greenhouse structures, and Evans has been tending to all manner of plants in there forever. By the time I came on the scene, well, what you see here is what there was. Pity, really. It was a grand estate that, in its day, could rival most in the historic district."

"That's why the gardener is so important to our study, then," I offered. "I really would like to spend more time with him before we lose all the light in the garden. What time does he end his workday?"

"Oh, I wouldn't worry your pretty little head about him. He stays around most all the time, except when he goes shopping or wherever he goes in the evening. Otherwise, he's always here, though…at least until the end of the year, when he'll have to find other accommodations. The commission said it's time for him to move on. Why all the interest in the old man?"

I blanched at Simon's callous remarks. "He might have some interesting thoughts about the plants we're working with during the garden's renovations."

We followed the brick walkway with its herringbone pattern to the back entrance, which sat a flight of stairs higher than ground level. Under those steps were three more steps down to the servants' entrance, again symmetrical in presentation. Simon gestured for me to follow him down these lower steps to enter the mansion.

I dawdled at the top of the steps while Simon fumbled with the key to the door. "Forgive the sandbags down here," he said, pointing to sandbags lining the door's threshold to the servants' entrance. "This spring's been a wet one, and we didn't want the house to sustain more water damage."

Noting the greenish cast on the sandbags and the brickwork under the stairs, I surmised there had to be lots of water down there. Thankfully, at that moment, Jack jogged up to the house to join us. "Oh, look; here's Jack." I nodded in Jack's direction. For a split second, I felt like Stephanie must, every time she sees Jack: *Here comes my hero, Jaaaaack, to rescue me.* The relief I felt probably matched Simon's aggravation with the lock.

"This lock must need a little graphite," he said, sounding exasperated. "Maybe we could try a different door. There's an alarm on the front door, too, and the box to turn off the alarm is down here. That's why we always try to use this entrance."

"It's okay, Simon," Jack said, noting the look on my face. "We really must be heading back. It's been a long day for us, and I still have a ton of work to do at the office."

"You're right, Jack; it has been a long day." Simon again turned his focus on me. This time, however, he stepped between Jack and me, getting a little closer to my face than I liked. His body language was certainly sending a message to both of us. "Maybe you should stay the night. We could have dinner—it would be on me, of course. I know a great little restaurant…."

"That's awfully sweet of you to offer," Jack stepped forward so he would be by Simon's side and force Simon to look his way. "We really should be heading back to Winston-Salem, Lily. Have you seen all that you need to for this trip?"

"Yes, I think I have. Thank you so much for your hospitality. We'll take a rain check on the mansion tour. Bye, now!" I barely managed to keep myself from breaking into a run back to the car. Jack was right beside me the whole way. When we were out of earshot of Simon, I flinched. "He infuriates me." I tossed Jack the car keys as we approached my car.

"What happened?" Jack opened my door for me.

"I don't know—he seems so callous and uncaring toward Evans. Plus, he was flirting with me, and rude to you. Throw the three attributes into the pot and it's a nasty stew I didn't care anything for today. Thanks for showing up when you did. I was getting a little concerned about being alone with him in the house."

Jack closed my door and went around to the driver's side. As he got in and closed his door, he looked at me. "You don't think he'd try anything, do you?"

"I wasn't interested in finding out. Thanks to you, I didn't have to."

"You are welcome," Jack said. "What a slime bag." He started up the car as he recounted some of our conversation with Evans. "He's done a masterful job of recording everywhere he has searched on the grounds. He gave me this sketch," Jack said as he pulled a folded piece of paper from his shirt pocket and handed it to me. "You know he loves this place."

"I can see that. I think it's been more than his job. It's been his calling to tend to these gardens all these years. It's a shame he has to leave."

"Leave? When? Why?"

"At the end of the year. Simon said the commission thought it best that he 'retire' and move off the grounds. I guess that means they'll bring in their own band of gardeners. That's why he came to me—to give the journal to me. He's running out of time to find the brooch."

"I wonder if he realizes that if he sells it, the brooch may not be worth much—or at least not enough to continue paying for the assistance Julia is getting," Jack said. "Those places are expensive!"

I thought about the costume jewelry of rhinestones I had bought that morning. They were copies of some incredible designs, but they weren't the real deal. If the brooch Evans bought for Julia contained diamonds, opals, and platinum—well, that might be worth a whole lot more than what Jack thought it might be worth. "I don't know, Jack; the brooch sounded pretty intricate to me. And with today's prices of gold and platinum being what they are, it may be worth a small fortune."

"Either way, it seems to have disappeared forever. Maybe Julia didn't put it in the garden after all. Maybe she hocked it for cash for her getaway."

"I don't think she'd do that. As young as she was, she probably would have wanted to keep such a piece. Jewelry isn't something women let go of easily." I thought of my overflowing jewelry box at home.

"He must have other funds…maybe he invested the ransom money all those years ago," I conjectured. "I bet that's the source of funds for Julia's care now."

"If that's the case, then he did right by her in the end, didn't he?"

"I guess, in an odd sort of way, he did. He may have been dishonest with her, but he was honorable." I reminded Jack of his earlier comments to Evans.

"Yeah, uh, sorry about that. I just called it the way I saw it."

"It's okay, Jack. It was a fair assessment. Julia was dishonest, too, but it's really not up to us to judge either of them at this point." Judging others is easier than fixing ourselves, I silently reminded myself. Looking over the sketch of the gardens where Evans had searched for the brooch, I was struck by how thorough he had been. The garden schematic showed where the fountain was in relation to his own caretaker's cottage, as well as the greenhouse, the main mansion, and the walls bordering the property. Large circles with jagged edges represented trees, and smaller circles represented bushes. Notes indicated a long boxwood hedge separating his cottage from the rest of the grounds as well as many other species. Evans had marked where other structures had stood when Julia lived in the house. On top of the garden schematic was a grid, faintly drawn in blue pencil. A large red X was drawn in most of the squares, which I took to mean spots where Evans had made unsuccessful digs. Interestingly, the grounds didn't appear pockmarked by the excavations indicated on this schematic. Evans had done a great job of covering up the holes he must have dug over nearly the entire estate. Unlike so many of the gardening layouts I'd studied during the course of the restoration, this drawing represented a lover's caress, something only someone with firsthand knowledge of a garden would draw. It also showed me something I'd not noticed before.

"Jack, I know where the brooch is. We have to go back."

Jack looked at me warily. "Does this include breaking and entering or some other crime?"

"Quite possibly. Turn the car around."

# Chapter Fifteen

When we drove by the Norton-Grace Mansion for the second time that day, the main gate was closed. Jack easily found a parking spot on the street around the corner from the main entrance. Tourists only visited this section of town during daylight hours, though I surmised that back in Julia's day, party guests would have parked in every available space on the street.

To Jack's amusement, I pulled two small flashlights from the back of my always prepared car. "What?" I asked.

"Who do you think we're going to encounter in there—Julia's ghost?"

"Maybe," I answered in a low voice. I shut the trunk of my car as quietly as I could manage and handed Jack a flashlight.

In the gathering darkness, Jack and I made our way around the north wall to the service entrance and hopped over the thigh-high wall. "We should probably let Evans know we're here," I whispered.

Jack tapped me lightly on the shoulder with his flashlight. "Why are we whispering?"

Glaring at him, I pushed his flashlight away from my shoulder. "Because I feel like it, okay?"

He smiled one of those smiles he shares so readily. Bowing slightly, he mouthed, "Sorry."

"There's the groundskeeper's cottage." I turned my light on the small structure at the opposite side of the garden. To reach it, we walked past the greenhouse and across the open expanse of the garden in full view of the house. Had he been paying attention, Evans could have witnessed almost anything happening in the garden. I knocked gently at first, but then louder when my knocking failed to raise an answer.

"Evans?" I pushed the door open and shined my flashlight inside the main room. "What happened here?"

Jack brushed by me into the topsy-turvy room. A fallen bookcase with books askew everywhere and a lamp knocked off a side table met our gaze. Jack rushed to an open door of the adjoining room, then looked back at me. "It's empty. There's nobody here."

That old feeling of dread rose in my throat again like bile. "The greenhouse?" I said as I turned toward the door to leave.

Jack followed. We hugged the garden's perimeter wall to the remaining greenhouse where Evans had shared his tale with us earlier.

"Evans?" I called. A soft groan drifted from the corner. Seconds later, we found him in a heap on the floor. A nasty-looking gash ran an inch across his forehead, though the blood flow didn't stop there. Quickly looking around the greenhouse, I found a roll of paper towels that would have to do. As Jack and I approached him, Evans put his hands up in protest.

"I tried to stop him, but he got so angry."

"Who? Who's here?" Jack blurted.

His brilliant blue eyes brimming with tears, Evans said quietly, "I can't…."

Jack carefully helped him stand, but Evans wavered and started to fall again. Jack helped him to a chair in the corner. "We'll call for help."

"No, please. I don't want trouble."

"Looks like trouble found you," I said, grabbing a gardening trowel as I bolted for the door.

Jack was close on my heels. "What do you think you're doing? You can't just…."

"What?" I swung around to face him. "Go defend a man who clearly needs defending? If you're not going to help, then stay out of my way." I broke into a run, my small flashlight's beam of light trained in front of me. I quickly searched the side of the greenhouse for anyone who shouldn't be there, then toward the house. My flashlight's beam was too puny to cast much light over there, but I didn't see any movement. Whoever had attacked Evans must have fled.

Back on task, I made my way to the fountain. I heard footsteps close behind me in the dark and smiled. Jack was on my side after all. He had my back, and I was glad for it since I had no idea whether whoever attacked Evans was still out here in the darkened garden with us. I looked for the entrance to the spiraling path encircling the old fountain that Evans had so neatly marked on his graph of attempted excavations. Following it closely, I shined my light along its edge and found what I was searching for—the one clue Evans had missed all these years.

Kneeling down, I used the trowel to loosen a large clump of small primrose plants out of the ground. Digging furiously, I felt the point of the trowel strike something hard. I followed the edges of it with the point of the trowel and my fingers. I dug away loose dirt until I could see what I guessed to be the top of an old cigar box, it's formerly brilliant colors faded by age and soil.

Feeling Jack standing right behind me, I felt a moment of elation at finding a treasure lost to the years. Keeping my voice in check, so as not to cause alarm, I spoke. "It's here, Jack. Right where she said it would be." I reached down to brush off the last of the soil, and then I coaxed the box top open. "Jack, shine you're light on this."

A bright light shined for an instant on a pale silk cloth—I guessed a handkerchief—then flew away high overhead and swooped down toward the ground beside me like an angry bird. Instinctively, I tucked my head and rolled on the ground in time to see a figure swing a flashlight at the spot where my head had been only seconds before. In an instant, I thrust my foot between my assailant's legs and scissor-kicked him to the ground. Leaping on top of him, I placed a direct palm strike to his sternum.

The yelp my attacker let out sounded much higher than Jack's yelp when we had sparred a week earlier. I grabbed the flashlight from my helpless attacker's hands as he lay there clutching his chest. Shining it in his face, I gasped. Simon Hester blinked furiously in the harsh light.

"Get off me!" he shrieked like a girl.

Jack ran up beside me. "You okay, Lily?" Then, seeing Simon writhing underneath me, he shouted. "You!" Jack helped me up first, then pulled Simon to his feet. Jack kept one arm on Simon's shoulder, ready to punch him back down in the dirt if needed. Jack stood tense at my side. "What the—"

I cut him off. "Simon was after this." I carefully opened the silk wrapping. The brooch I pulled out shone brilliantly under all three of our flashlights. I'm not an expert on Art Nouveau-styled jewelry, but I could see this brooch was an incredible work of art. Given what Evans had told us about it, I could easily imagine what Julia's reaction might have been upon receiving it. Filling up nearly all of the palm of my hand was an amazing array of jewels, yellow gold, and platinum that was nearly three inches long and two inches wide. Organic-looking compositions of smaller diamonds clustered around larger ones like petals of flowers, with tendrils of small diamonds and a green gem rising up to embrace an open flower made of several shapes and colors of natural-edged opals. It was, in a word, sensational.

"Thanks for finding it for me," Simon said, collecting what was left of his dignity as he brushed himself off. He reached for the brooch, but Jack quickly blocked his arm with a swift downward strike of his hand. He grabbed Simon in a headlock.

"Not so fast."

"That brooch is mine!" Simon shouted, Jack's arm still tight around his throat.

"Simon," panted Jack, holding him in a headlock, "the brooch isn't yours."

Simon grabbed again for the brooch, but Jack was ready for him. "Oh, no, you don't." Jack released Simon from his headlock and stepped between Simon and me.

"But it belongs to me," Simon persisted.

"We'll see about that," I said as I placed the brooch gently back in its cloth and then gathered the cigar box for the brooch's protection. Using the trowel, I replanted the clump of plants I'd pulled out of the ground as best I could in the dark. Perhaps no one but a gardener would notice the plants had been disturbed. I could only hope nobody else would be searching for this treasure, for the sake of what was left of the garden.

"Evans is hurt," said Jack. "We should probably get the police."

"Don't...don't do that." Simon raised both hands in a pleading motion. "I didn't mean for him to get hurt. It was just after you two left. I finally managed to get the mansion's downstairs door to unlock and went inside to make sure everything in the house was as it should be. From an upstairs window, I watched Evans as he closed up the greenhouse, and then locked the gates to the property like he does every night. From my vantage point, I could see everything that was going on in the garden. It made me wonder what you two were up to: you've been here time and time again to see the gardens, so I figured that another special trip just to speak with Evans must have been important. I wondered what he could have told you that you didn't know already, so I had to find out what he said.

"When I saw the lights turn on in his cottage, I walked over to it and knocked on the door. I guess he didn't hear me—he is a little hard of hearing—so I opened the door. When I called out his name, he still didn't hear me, so I approached him in his kitchen and tapped him on the shoulder. I surprised him and he fell over a chair and hit his head on a table. When he pulled himself up by a nearby bookcase, the case fell over and hit more furniture in the room. I was trying to help him, but he pushed me away and I fell over another chair and knocked a lamp onto the floor. He left in a hurry, and I followed him through the garden to the greenhouse. I was merely trying to talk to him when you two showed up. It was just an accident. Please don't involve the police."

"What did you want to talk to him about?" Jack snapped. Clearly, he was still in fight mode, even though his breathing had returned to normal…nearly.

"That, of course," Simon said, pointing at the cigar box I clutched. "It belongs to me." He took a deep breath. "I suppose you want to know why. Once you hear what he did to me, I'm sure you'll agree I'm entitled to it."

"You can talk while we're walking," Jack said. "We need to go see about Evans." He shoved Simon in the back in a not-so-gentle manner. I could tell it would take a bit for him to calm down.

Simon sighed deeply before speaking. "I supposed he knew where it was all along, but whenever I asked him, he became evasive. I needed to find it, so I went to the caretaker's cottage about a year ago. He wasn't home, so I took the opportunity to search the place. All I found was Julia's journal, or diary, or whatever you want to call it. I intended to take it home to make copies of every page so I could study them later—I was sure they held some clue as to where the brooch was. I was right on that point. I miscalculated my timing, though. I was reading the journal when I heard his keys in the door. I ripped out the last couple of pages, hoping they would tell me where I needed to look. I got out of there with a flimsy excuse to Evans, but my visit must have shaken him up sufficiently that he felt the journal was no longer safe in his possession. I studied the journal's last pages at home, but I found absolutely nothing of value. I even took the pages to a friend of mine at the university. She's a horticulturalist on the staff there. I showed her the pages under the guise of wanting an expert opinion on plants that should be added to the gardens, which seemed believable, given my position in town and on this project. She told me quite a lot about what was on the pages. In fact, I had a newfound respect for Evans—it didn't take long for me to figure out what he was up to.

"The very next day, the commission had a meeting and your friend Macy was there. Evans must have sensed she was in charge of the project, not to mention that she wasn't from Columbia, so he must have decided to give her the journal for safekeeping then. I saw her walk through the garden with Evans. She was excited about something, and she kept pointing to one plant or another. Next thing I heard was that the gal was dead. I always wondered if Evans was capable of something so deviant. After that day, I knew he was. He killed her because she probably knew too much. With her out of the way, he got Julia's journal back and was free to search the garden again."

I hesitated to tell Simon about my earlier conversation with Evans, but he needed to know the truth. "Simon, Macy died of a heart attack. Evans didn't murder her, or anyone else as far as I know."

"But the notations of plant toxicity—yes, I did see those in the journal, and the horticulturalist confirmed my suspicions," said Simon. "Sure, he knew what he was doing."

"He could have, but he didn't kill her. Macy had a bad reaction to several of the plants she was touching as she talked to Evans in the greenhouse that day you saw her. It was the equivalent of contact dermatitis that went terribly wrong. He said when she hit the ground, he fished out the journal from her bag and then he called for help. If he had intended for her to die, he wouldn't have called anyone so quickly."

Jack nodded his head in agreement.

"Either way, he searched for that jewelry for decades," Simon said in a huff. "He never found it because Julia didn't really want him to. She hid it from him before leaving town. She made a choice not to wear it or to take it with her. That action speaks volumes about her true feelings for him."

"You can't possibly know what she was feeling, or why she did what she did," I rose to Julia's defense. "Maybe she had every intention of coming back for it. Maybe she felt it was such a stunning piece of jewelry that it would be easily traced and her secret identity would have been discovered. She was scared, Simon."

"Ah, but I do know what she was feeling. I read the last few pages of her journal, the ones I ripped out," Simon gloated. "Something you apparently haven't had the pleasure of reading, I assume."

"What did the pages say?" I tried to control the anger rising in my chest.

"Simply everything she was feeling the day she ran. She felt horrible for what she did, though she never committed to paper what exactly that was. She wrote that she was leaving the journal behind because she couldn't bear to read it again, and she hoped that she would be forgiven in time, especially by the people she cared for the most. She said she never wanted to come back again to a place filled with so many memories, both good and bad. And finally, she wrote that she had buried the brooch in her secret garden, the one Evans gave to her. She wrote that she buried it like a dead person in the dirt because she felt like she didn't deserve it after what she had done. She said she left enough clues within her diary's pages for Evans to find it and to do with it what he wanted. The old fool."

Jack spun Simon around to face him before we entered the greenhouse. "If you and Evans aren't on the best of terms these days, how is it you came to know about the brooch in the first place?"

Simon laughed. "He didn't tell you, did he?"

"Tell us what?" Jack crossed his arms over his chest.

"He's my father."

The shock probably registered on my face. "Your father?"

"Yep, Evans is my dear old dad. I always thought he would give that brooch to me as my inheritance. It's probably worth a bit of money now, given the prices of precious metals these days, so you could save us all a lot of trouble and just hand it over." Simon held out his hand for the cigar box.

"Nothing doing, Simon." Jack was in his face again, measuring his words carefully. "Simon, you didn't answer my question, so I'll ask it again: if you and your dad are not on the greatest terms with each other, then how did you even know about the journal and the brooch? I seriously doubt Evans would have shared the journal with you."

"Because Julia showed that brooch to my mother soon after Evans gave it to her. Julia was so excited about it that she couldn't keep it to herself. My mother was Julia's best friend."

My mouth was hanging open large enough for a jet to fly in. "Mary—from the journal? The Mary who went to the beach with her? Julia's best friend, Mary?"

"Yes. *That* Mary. Evans—my dad—showed my mother the brooch he planned to give to Julia in hopes of getting Mother to encourage Julia to accept his advances as a suitor. He wanted to court her properly, and he felt sure the brooch would seal it for him. Julia showed Mary the brooch to gloat about it and having landed Evans when she clearly knew my mother was in love with him. Her diary said so. My mother had always had a crush on Evans, it seems. She thought for sure Julia would see how devoted Evans was to her once Julia saw that brooch and learned how hard he had worked to pay for it. Though it upset my mother, she was willing to do what she felt was best for Julia's future with him. Unfortunately, as her actions demonstrated, Julia had another plan in mind. My dad wouldn't see Julia for the troubled person she was. He even helped Julia after a boy at a party got a cup of spiked punch that Julia must have doctored. The toxic plants she marked in the journal, remember? Didn't she even consider that she might have killed someone? She was evil!"

The article Jack shared with me earlier told a sad tale of how one of Julia's friends, the one Evans had called a suitor, fell to the ground. "He survived, though, Simon," I offered, "with nothing more than something akin to a stomach bug."

"Doesn't matter that he lived. What does matter is it shows just how evil she was. The news was all over town. I'm sure you've scanned the old newspaper articles and read the same things I did. My poor mother—Mary Hester—was so upset when Julia disappeared without saying goodbye. Sometime after that, Evans showed up on my mother's doorstep. I guess he was turning to her for comfort at that point, but he wasn't over Julia. No way."

Now that he'd started, Simon wasn't letting up. His hate-laced words continued to spill out of him. "My mother showed him comfort in more ways than one, apparently. It didn't seem to matter, though. My father was blind to who Julia really was, what she was capable of doing. He was so blind he was willing to help her leave town, to run away from the trouble she'd caused. Of course, she lied to him, probably like she'd done to him since the first day they met. She probably told him she'd let him know when she was settled. And he believed her, the fool. My mother willingly took him on the rebound. She was thrilled at the prospect of having a family with him. She did love him dearly, even though she knew Julia had his heart. Since Julia never contacted them again, Mother thought that old romance was in the past. But he just couldn't let it go—he couldn't let Julia go. When I was young, he left us to go in search of Julia. And my mother still forgave him for his idiocy. All those years, when my father was pining after Julia, Mom loved him still. Since he's been back at this property, he has been searching for the brooch all this time, and Julia's of absolutely no help to anyone: she's in a nursing home with dementia or something like it," Simon said.

"Nice story, Simon, but it doesn't mean that you should be the one to keep the brooch," Jack said. "It doesn't belong to you. It still belongs to Julia."

Simon clicked his tongue on the inside of his mouth like a scolding parent. "He never could get past Julia to see how awesome a person my mom was. My mother died two years ago, but not before telling me about the journal and the brooch. I should have it since I've had precious little from that man all these years. He's as guilty as Julia is for wrecking a lot of lives."

"Simon, the only thing he's guilty of is loving Julia," I said as I gently touched his arm. "You're missing out on time with him because of your pride, so it's partly your fault that you haven't had a relationship with him all these years. Yeah, I realize you think he made a mistake by leaving you and your mother alone, but he's human. We're all human. Perhaps it's time for you to forgive him?"

Simon ripped his arm away from mine. "You have *no idea* how hard my mother had to work to raise me, to support us. Her friends turned their backs on her because she'd been hanging out with 'the help' and her family disowned her when she got pregnant with me. After he disgraced her by leaving town in search of Julia, she worked two jobs to support us and to move us to a better neighborhood where I would meet the 'right' people in town. She sold everything she had to pay for me to go to college," Simon bellowed.

Believe me, I did know how hard it was to raise a child alone. But Simon obviously wanted to wallow in his pity. I just listened.

"Over the years, I've kept up with the renovations of this mansion and the gardens. I hoped one day to uncover the journal's secrets. I hoped to be the one to find that brooch you're holding. I spent countless hours volunteering to weed garden beds, divide plants, and rebuild rock walls in search of it. I even finagled my way onto the commission's list of architects to vie for the project so I could be in charge of the mansion's renovations…all of it just to have one more try at finding that brooch. I searched the greenhouse for Julia's journal on more than one occasion, too. And when I saw Macy that day in the greenhouse with my father, I figured the journal would eventually find its way to your firm. I followed him all the way from Columbia that day he brought it to you. I knew what he was doing, so it was only a matter of time before I figured out you had it. That's why I dated that bubble-headed receptionist of yours—hoping to find it in the office. I even searched your office after one of our meetings, but it wasn't there."

"You low life!" Jack lunged at Simon, but I stepped in between Simon and Jack, though I really did want Jack to have a go at him. Simon deserved it for using Stephanie and for trespassing in my office.

Jack backed off only to appease my pleading look.

"Simon, how did Mary—your mother—know the brooch was here?" I asked.

"She told me she had visited Julia one afternoon at that facility. In a moment of clarity, Julia told her about the brooch being hidden somewhere in the garden, and Julia went on and on about how beautiful it was, with clusters of diamonds surrounding a huge grouping of opals. She'd hoped to show it to Mother, she said. I guess she didn't remember sharing it with her long ago," Simon said. "When my mom asked Julia to be more specific about its location in the garden, Julia was 'gone' again. My mom actually sent me here to find it so she could give it back to Julia to mend the rift between them. Can you believe it?" Simon said in a low voice. "The things my mother did for Julia astound me. Seems she loved Julia like a sister, too."

I could sense Simon was winding down. "She was doing the right thing then, Simon. The brooch was Julia's. It was a gift from Evans, long before you were born, regardless of subsequent decisions he made or actions he took with your mother. You have to let go."

"He should have given it to my mom."

"He did what he thought was right. Now, we have to do the same thing. Come on. Let's go see about your dad." I offered my hand to Simon.

"Come on, Simon," said Jack in agreement. "Let's go visit your dad. You know, you could still mend the relationship if you wanted to."

"No thanks. I don't want anything to do with him. He turned his back on us. I'm just returning the favor."

"That's your choice, Simon, but it'll be your loss. When he's gone, you won't have the opportunity to tell him how you feel."

"Oh, he knows how I feel, all right. He knows." Simon stormed off.

"Wonder if he's going to remain on the project team," Jack said with a sigh as we watched Simon's figure dissolve into the shadows near the grand old house. "He's a damn good architect."

# Chapter Sixteen

After tending to the cut on Evans' forehead with several stick-on bandages, Jack and I helped Evans for the rest of the evening to restore order to his small cottage. He offered us each a cup of tea. While the water heated in a kettle, I found two cans of soup and some crackers to serve up for a light supper. Evans seemed grateful for the help and for the company.

"I can't thank you enough for finding that brooch," he said between tastes of soup. "Julia did like it when I gave it to her. I hope she'll appreciate it again."

"Are you going to sell it, Evans?" Clearly, Jack's mouth was working faster than his mind. I gave him a sharp kick under the table. "What? What did I say?"

Evans smiled and put down his mug of tea. "I haven't decided yet. For years, I thought I would, but seeing it again reminds me of how lovely it looked on Julia. The staff at the nursing home does a good job of taking care of the residents, but I've heard tales of things going missing. And if Julia doesn't want it or doesn't enjoy wearing it, well, there's no point in keeping it, I suppose. I'll sell it if she doesn't want it anymore. Amazingly, it's worth quite a bit of money now. A few years ago, I did some research on one of the local library's computers. I found two others very similar to it, and they were recently auctioned or sold for over thirty thousand dollars!" Evans eyes lit up as he spoke. "But I intended it for Julia when I bought it, and I want to make sure she has a chance to see it again. It's hard for me to watch her in this condition. Some days, she's quite lucid, and can hold court among the other residents in the place where she lives, just like the old days. It's like nothing's changed, you know? Other times, well, she doesn't seem to recognize me. I visit her every day, and I feel so blessed on her good days."

"Did she ever tell you what she did for all those years before you found her?" Jack asked. "I mean, I know you said she was a waitress, but how could she have not known what really happened? She could have found out that the fellow only ended up in the hospital rather than dying. She could have come home a lot sooner."

"I've tried to talk with her about that so many times, but each time, I get the same reply. She just keeps saying that it was her fault. And yes, she did serve up a fairly potent drink at the party that day, but it was an accident that he drank it. I mean, it wasn't meant for him, anyway. Who knows if Mary would have reacted to it in the same way? Mary and I both touched the same plants often when we sat or gardened with Julia on a daily basis. Truth is, I feel fairly certain I'd built up an immunity to their…" Evans searched for the right words, "side effects. I looked for her for years so I could tell her the truth about what had happened, and to let her know it was just an accident. Mary never knew, of course, that the drink Julia prepared was intended for her. When I found Julia, I assured her that her motive behind the incident would always be our little secret. My hope, of course, was that she'd come out of hiding and come home to me."

"But weren't you concerned for your own safety after she showed what she could do with plants?" Jack wouldn't let up, so I kicked him under the table a bit harder this time. He just glared at me, not understanding what that kick was for, either.

Evans ignored our little under-the-table interaction and continued. "I forgave her—I know I may have been a bit of pest when we were younger, and I suppose she thought I was toying with her affections. She was so upset that I acted the gentleman and sent her home on that one night when she really didn't want me to be that way. And since she felt I was having an affair with Mary, well, I can see how much she must have cared for me to act that way. Yes, I realize she was…troubled. But I've never wanted to turn my back on her. Julia had my heart from the first day we met, and knowing that she loved me to that degree, well, I can't possibly know how very hurt she must have felt thinking that I was interested in Mary at the time...hurt enough to want to injure Mary. We never told Mary or anyone else for that matter, either. No one ever knew, and the party hosts thought the fellow just had a stomach bug. It wasn't until the police showed up later, trying to figure out what happened to Julia when she disappeared, that anybody ever wondered, you know?

Forensic science wasn't as sophisticated as it is today, so it would have been hard to sort out."

"Why didn't Mary drink what was intended for her?" Jack asked, and then cautiously looked at me. Fair question. I refrained from kicking him.

"That boy was a bit of a bully. He muscled his way into most situations, and clearly intended to do the same this time, asking Julia to dance when she obviously was standing so close to me. I think Mary saw him coming, and wanted to give Julia and me a chance to be together on the dance floor like I told Mary I'd like to do. Mary gave her drink to the fellow in hopes of keeping him with her at the table so Julia and I could have a chance on the dance floor. Sadly, it didn't work out that way, as you two now know. That fellow always had a way of making everything about *him.* The attention he must have gotten in the hospital after collapsing with a stomach bug must have thrilled him," said Evans, smiling.

"What about the ransom money?" Jack sounded parental, and I gave him another swift kick under the table. "Ouch!"

"Julia's parents had more money than they ever knew what to do with, frankly. I figured they wouldn't notice the small amount we asked for. Over the years, I managed to put a little in a variety of banks around South Carolina and in Georgia so as not to call attention to the total sum being deposited. Most of it I hid here." He rose from the table and limped to the floor-to-ceiling bookcase. He removed a large leather-bound book and brought it back to the table. Slowly, he opened the cover of the old book titled, *The History of Gardening.* Inside were pages with their centers cut out. A few bills remained within their hiding spot, firmly secured by the weight of a stone arranged on a spring somewhat like a mousetrap. "There were other books I fixed up just like this one. I didn't want to keep it all in one place, you know. I used the interest off the money in the banks and in various investments to help pay for Julia's care all these years. I've never used a cent of it on myself, I swear." He sat back in his chair, quiet for a moment. "I hope you won't judge me too harshly."

"Seems to me you've suffered enough for your…decisions," I said, patting his hand on the table. I imagined the statute of limitations might be called into play if Simon ever sorted out what happened with the money, but since he thought Julia ran away with it, well, I felt what he didn't know wouldn't hurt him.

"Thank you for understanding and for your help in finding the brooch." Evans squeezed my hand in return. "I truly couldn't have done it without you." We both looked at Jack, who sat silently in his chair.

"What?"

"Don't you have anything to say?"

"I was afraid I'd get kicked again."

Evans and I laughed as Jack rubbed his shin under the table.

• • •

Jack volunteered to clean up the dishes while I helped Evans sort out the items that had fallen on the floor during his earlier spill. I felt sure he'd benefit from a trip to the local hospital and perhaps a few stitches to his forehead, but he insisted it was just a scratch. "I don't want to leave my cottage tonight," he said as we picked up the last of the books that had scattered on the floor when he hit the table. "No, I think I'll just stay here. A good night's sleep will help."

"Evans, Simon said the commission felt it best you move on at the end of the year. Where will you go?"

"Not far from here," he said. "I've given it a great deal of thought, and I agree with the commission that it's time for me to leave. They have an outstanding crew of people working on some of the other gardens at properties in the historic district who will take over the task of maintaining whatever plants you decide should be planted." He took a seat in what I imagined was his favorite chair, given how worn the striped fabric was on the upholstered arms. "I'm going to join Julia when the time comes. The place where she lives has a wing for people like me who don't have what she has. Truly, I'm tired of keeping this place up." He motioned with his arm to his tiny cottage. "I'm tired of eating my meals alone. No, I think it would be nice to have some company. And on the days when I don't feel like talking to anyone but Julia, I'll just go and sit with her. See, it's a way for us finally to be together."

"That sounds like a great idea, Evans." I hesitated to bring up the subject of money, but I plunged ahead as a dutiful daughter might. "Are you sure you can afford it?"

"I've been careful with my money. The wages I earned on my own from several different jobs I've held down at the same time might have been meager on their own, but because I combined them, and invested them wisely, the investments have grown so that I won't ever want for anything. Neither will Julia."

"So you don't need to sell the brooch for cash?"

"Not at this point, I don't. I know that's what Simon would have done with it. He's so…closed minded. He just can't understand how I feel about Julia."

I didn't want to follow him down that rabbit hole of thought about Simon, but I sensed there was a need for closure between the two of them. "You know, it's not too late for you to talk to him about the way you feel. Perhaps he needs to hear how you felt about his mother, most of all."

"Mary was a dear, sweet friend who listened to a foolish man like me. I don't know what she ever saw in me, but I saw her kindness when I couldn't find a friend anywhere else. She was always willing to listen, and she wasn't the least bit judgmental. I know some of her high society friends snubbed her when we got together, but she didn't seem to care. She was so happy when she learned she was pregnant with Simon. I did the best I could, really. I tried to be a family man, a good mate, and a good father. My heart just wasn't in it, though, and Mary knew it. It was actually Mary who encouraged me to go look for Julia. Her kindness was her greatest strength."

"She didn't tell Simon that part," Jack came into the room, drying his hands on a towel slung over his shoulder. "Simon is under the impression that you abandoned Mary and him to go in search of Julia."

Evans started to shake. "Nothing could be further from the truth! Mary spent countless hours helping me write up classified ads to send to various papers around the country. This was back before the days of the Internet, so we did the best we could getting notices of Julia's disappearance out there. Why, Mary believed as much as I did that Julia should come home and make amends with her family. I swore I'd give the money back to her papa when she came home because Mary and I didn't touch any of it. We both worked hard to make a living for ourselves, but…."

"It's okay, Evans." Jack sat down on the edge of the coffee table in front of him. "Sometimes, relationships just don't work out for one reason or another." He paused for a second. "What happened with Simon? He seems so hateful."

"I guess that's my fault," Evans said. "He grew up without me around most of the time. And when he was old enough to understand a little of it—I'd guess he was not quite a teenager—well, he didn't think what his mother and I did was right. Simon and I fought constantly, and Mary couldn't stand to hear it any longer, so she agreed with me that I should leave for good. I found odd jobs when I would be in a place searching for Julia, and continued to send Mary a bit of money to help out when I could, but I decided at that point to put all my energies into finding Julia. By the time I brought

Julia back to Columbia with me, Mary had developed cancer. Mary was as pleased to have Julia back as I was, and the two of them did have some good times together before Julia got to the point of needing to be moved into the assisted living place. When Mary passed away two years ago, Simon was furious with me for leaving in the first place, and even perhaps for coming back. Simon just didn't understand the relationship I had with his mother. I genuinely did care for Mary, but Julia, well, she had my heart from the very first day we met. I couldn't change the way I felt, but I guess Simon thought I should have been able to turn it off and on like a light switch."

"Don't I wish emotions were that easy to control," Jack said. "Life would be so much easier, and a whole lot less messy, if we could control our feelings." He turned and looked directly at me. For the first time under his gaze, I felt a little uncomfortable.

"It's like I told Simon earlier—it's his loss if he doesn't try to befriend you," Jack added. "The great mystery is over, you have the brooch, and all that's left to be settled is his feelings toward you."

"Thank you for saying so, Jack," Evans said, rubbing his eyes gently, "but I fear he won't see it that way."

"You must be tired, Evans. Let's see if we can't all get some rest. Jack, do you mind?" I pointed to the floor to suggest what the sleeping arrangements would be. I assumed he'd be a gentleman and give me the couch.

"Not on your life, Lily. You won't catch me on the floor when there's a perfectly good hammock out back.

I saw it when we were sneaking around the back of the house earlier today."

"We weren't sneaking, Jack." I turned to Evans. "We were just being cautious."

"Call it what you like, but whispering in the night while walking around a gated property with flashlights after jumping over a wall to get in sure felt like sneaking around to me."

Jack jumped up from his perch on the coffee table and dashed back to the kitchen before I could speak. I suppose this unexpected trip to Columbia had included all those things he just mentioned. I wondered whether my son would be proud—or mortified. Perhaps I wouldn't tell him about this little adventure after all.

"That hammock has been out there for some time," Evans spoke, his voice sounding tired, "but it's still serviceable. Let me find you an extra blanket and pillow." Evans stood slowly and made his way to the cottage's bedroom. A few minutes later, he emerged with arms full of a comforter and pillow. Jack offered to take them from Evans, but Evans shook his head. "You are both my guests, so I will take care of the accommodations. Sorry I can't offer more in the way of comfort."

"You're kidding, right?" Jack followed him to the door. "That hammock is going to feel like a bed at a four-star hotel to me. And did you see the stars out tonight? I can't wait to stargaze. It's been a personal hobby of mine for years, and it's been a while since I've had the opportunity. See, I camped as I hiked the entire Appalachian

Trail," he started his repertoire. "I remember like it was yesterday the time I met Colin Fletcher, the author of several incredible books on hiking. I had read each and every one of them, of course...."

Jack's repertoire was new to Evans, but not to me, so I tuned out his told-too-often hiking stories. I pulled the brooch out of my bag, and turned it over in my hands. *It could do with a little cleaning,* I thought. In the kitchen, I found a soft cloth under the sink sitting on a small can of silver polish. Wary of what it might do to the brooch's finish, I opted instead for a dab of dishwashing soap and warm water. Gently, I cleaned the brooch, careful not to leave a soapy residue on any of the tiny prongs holding the gemstones in place. The brooch was a work of art in any age. I could see why Julia would have been thrilled to get it, but for the life of me, I couldn't fathom intentionally hiding something so precious in the dirt. Julia must have been distraught to take the perilous actions she did all those years ago. Her intense love for Evans was only matched by his for her.

I wondered what it would be like to be loved that intensely. Not just lusted after, the way my ex-husband seemed to lust after everything in a skirt that moved—the way he once did me, I supposed—but truly, deeply, and eternally loved. Aside from my parents' protective love, I couldn't say I'd ever had that kind of a relationship with anyone. But who was I trying to kid? It's been so long since I was in a relationship of any kind, lust-filled, love, or whatever. My marriage was a train wreck. Years of healing, and I'm still more than a little gun shy to consider attempting another relationship. But…Jack is different than my ex. He's solid, reliable, available, and seemingly interested in me. I still wonder if dating or going out or whatever it's called these days is the right thing to do. As coworkers, we get along most of the time, but still…what happens when we don't get along?

My head felt like it took a bad tumble from the high bars in this game of mental gymnastics with thoughts of Jack, so I decided I wouldn't give him another thought for the night. I dried the brooch carefully and then wrapped it in a washcloth before returning it to my bag. After a quick inspection of Jack's efforts at tidying up the kitchen, I turned in time to see Evans coming back through the door.

"Everything okay?" I called.

"Your friend is settled in just fine," Evans said. "Now I'm going to take care of you, too. I'll get an extra blanket and pillow from the shelf." He disappeared into his room and soon returned with a blanket and small pillow. "Are you sure you wouldn't be more comfortable in my room? I'm used to snoozing on my couch," he offered.

I shook my head in refusal. "I'll be just fine out here. Now, you get to bed. You're going to need your rest for tomorrow."

Evans looked closely at me. At first, I wasn't sure he heard me. Then, he said quietly, "I can hardly wait." He was sincere, I could tell. I watched as Evans slowly turned and entered his bedroom and closed his door.

*Neither can I.*

# Chapter Seventeen

Jack urged me to enter the plain room, devoid of color and decorations. It was not, however, devoid of character. Early-stage Alzheimer's patients mingled with other residents in various stages of health under the watchful eye of healthcare professionals. A keyboardist played songs from the 1940s and '50s, the residents' singing voices responding to notes of songs they remembered. A few gazes my way seemed to be filled with hope that I was there either with treats or news. Some looked at me as if in search of a name of someone long remembered but scarcely seen. Hesitating in the doorway, I scanned the room for the person I felt I should know on sight. Had it not been for Evans sitting quietly beside her, though, I may never have found Julia.

"You have a visitor, dear." Evans leaned over her wheelchair to announce my presence as I approached. He carefully wheeled her toward the open balcony door that led to a terrace. Surrounded by potted plants and bright blooms, he looked at me with those brilliant eyes beaming, nodding for me to come join them.

With a backward glance at Jack, I turned and slowly made my way through the group of disappointed residents.

"She seems calmest out here," he said quietly when I got close enough to see her. "I'm glad the weather held. Julia, you have company," he said again, putting a ruddy hand on her shoulder.

Slowly moving around the wheelchair, I took a seat on a curved concrete bench in front of her. Julia was as beautiful as I had imagined, despite her advanced years. Her long brown hair was braided and coiled in a loose bun. Streaks of white hair framed her delicate face, and her eyes were as bright as sapphires. They held a sad vacancy, though. Taking cues from Evans, I introduced myself as a friend. "Julia, it's good to see you. I've been working in your garden. You've done a marvelous job identifying the plants for me." From my bag, I pulled out a small potted Japanese lily with lavender blooms, whose sweet honey-like smell drifted like perfume. "I brought this plant to you as a gift."

Julia's eyes brightened, glistening with moisture at the edges. "Oh, Mary, you remembered! I thought everyone forgot my birthday this year. Mama said we couldn't go to the beach again, but I still had hopes. I wanted to collect more plants like the ones we got last year. Remember? I have three more empty spots to fill near the old fountain; then I think my masterpiece will be complete." She turned to Evans and grabbed his hand. "Isn't this exciting? We're going to have a party now." Julia's voice faded. She released Evans' hand as a dark shadow crossed her face and a scowl replaced her smile. "Why haven't you brought me anything, Evans? It's my birthday," she whimpered like a spoiled child might.

"He did, Julia; he just wanted it to be a surprise." I carefully pulled from my bag the small washcloth I'd borrowed from Evans' kitchen the night before and handed it to Evans. "Give it to her. It's okay. It's yours to give to her," I encouraged him.

Jack walked up behind Julia's wheelchair to watch as Evans gingerly opened the sides of the towel to reveal the sparkling brooch he offered to her so many years ago. With tears in his eyes, he handed it to her for a second time.

"Julia, I chose this especially for you," he said hoarsely. "I hope you like it."

"Oh, Evans, it's lovely. And I was beginning to wonder if you really cared. Thank you! Please, put it on me."

Evans knelt down to pin it on her dark green sweater. The hinged pin was as stiff as he seemed to be. With tears streaming down his face, he fumbled with the closing clasp.

I reached over and helped him secure the brooch in place. "Lovely. Julia, it suits you. Evans, you really outdid yourself this time," I said to him. I meant it, too. The brooch that he'd saved for years to buy sparkled in the morning sun.

Julia smiled. "Oh, thank you, Evans; it's just perfect. I love it! And…" she lowered her voice, "I love you, too."

Evans leaned over and kissed her on the cheek.

"Not in front of Mary, Evans," Julia teased. I could hear in that voice a hint of the kind of relationship they would have had all these years if not for that one decision Mary had made years before.

"It's okay, Julia; I won't tell. You and Evans are perfect for each other." I squeezed her hand and rose to leave. "Thank you, Evans."

Evans stood up and clamped my arm in his still-strong grip. "You have it all wrong. I should thank you for bringing my Julia back to me, if only for this moment."

Normally, I'm not one for tears, so when I felt hot moisture around my eyes, I smiled quickly and turned to go. "We'll show ourselves out." I looked at Jack, who nodded in agreement.

"Lily!" Julia called after me. "I had almost forgotten the name of this plant you gave me, but now I remember. It is a lily. Thank you, Mary. Evans and I will put it in the garden this afternoon, won't we, Evans?"

"Yes, Julia. Yes, of course we will." Evans raised his hand to us, a smile broadening across his weathered face. It was a look of gratitude I would never forget.

My step was lighter than it had been in months, and I felt relieved. Then I saw Simon sulking away down the corridor. I guessed he had followed us here and witnessed the entire exchange that just occurred between Julia and his father. Fearing another confrontation, my guard was up. I could feel Jack tense, but close to my side, as we walked out of the building a few steps behind Simon. He stopped as we reached the front doors of the building.

"It was the right thing to do, even though I don't like it," muttered Simon.

"Simon, I'm sorry about—"

Simon cut me off. "No need to apologize. I thought about what you said, and I saw with my own two eyes how much my father loves her still," he paused. "Thank you for bringing my old man such joy."

"Forgive him, Simon." It was all I could think to say. "Forgive him and get on with your life."

I knew I should heed my own words.

• • •

The drive home from Columbia was a quiet one. I was thankful Jack was driving because the emotions of the past twenty-four hours had worn me out. I was looking forward to a shower and a long nap. "Jack, thanks. Thanks for coming."

"Sure," said Jack, lost to his own thoughts.

"What's the matter?"

"What I don't understand is how you knew where to find the brooch. Evans and Simon had each searched for it, combing through every inch of that garden for years. Yet you just saunter in and locate it like Julia herself told you where it was."

"She did," I said, "in her journal. It took me a while to figure it out. At first, I thought the numbers running down the sides of the pages in her journal were quantities for each plant in the garden. But something my nieces said to me stuck with me. Most every plant follows a pattern in terms of the numbers of petals or seeds. They are mathematically perfect. Julia wasn't listing their quantities; she was listing their locations."

"Huh?"

"Are you familiar with Leonardo Bigollo?"

"Is he an Italian cook?"

"No, Jack, he wasn't. Bigollo was also known as Fibonacci, and he is considered one of the most talented mathematical minds of the Middle Ages. It was his idea to use Arabic numbers rather than Roman numerals."

"So?"

"So, he studied sequences of numbers, where each successive number is the sum of the two numbers that came before. Like one plus one equals two, and one plus two equals three. Two plus three equals five, and so on. You may not have noticed the curve in the wall of Julia's interior garden, but the plants inside were organized in a pattern." I dug into my glove compartment for a scrap of paper and sketched out the garden to show what I meant. "See? There was one peony originally in her garden, and beside it were two peace lilies." I turned the paper for Jack to glance at as he drove. "There were three hosta plants, then five hellebores next." I exaggerated the spiral to help Jack see the pattern. "See what I mean?"

I could feel the car swerve as Jack strained to see the drawing. "Jack! Eyes on the road!"

"You just told me to look!" Jack corrected course. "I see what you're saying; it's like the spiral chambers of a Nautilus shell."

"Exactly." I remembered the lovely pictures Ben shared with me. "Fibonacci's study is often called the 'golden ratio' or the 'golden mean,' and he demonstrated the regular frequency with which patterns repeat in nature…petals, seeds in a sunflower's center, and the spirals of chambered shells like the Nautilus shell. The next number in Julia's garden sequence should have been eight because that's the sum of the two numbers that come before it, meaning five and three. But the next plant grouping in the garden contains ten of the same species. I studied the commission's documentation and compared it to Julia's notes. In fact, I studied her journal for so long that I memorized them. When I realized it was not a quantity listing, but a sequence she was noting—"

"You knew exactly where to look," Jack finished my thoughts, "under the grouping of ten plants in the sequence. It should have been eight of the species, not ten."

"Correct. Evans and Simon couldn't find the brooch because they were not looking in the right place. The pattern was circular, like the petals on a dahlia or the chambers of the nautilus. When the golden ratio was out of sequence, I knew there was a problem. There could be only one answer as to the location of the item in question. I just didn't know what we were looking for until last night in the garden."

Jack smiled at me. It wasn't his teasing look, or his puppy-dog look. I interpreted it to be a look of admiration.

"Remind me to team up with you on the company scavenger hunt this summer. You're awesome at figuring out clues."

I smiled, too. "Actually, it was Julia who was smart enough to leave them for me. It's just so sad that she didn't see Evans for who he really was at first, and still is. She could have had a lovely life gardening with him all these years."

"And exactly who do you think he is?"

"A man who has loved Julia forever."

"True. He'll take good care of her, just as he always has. Hey, this calls for a celebration," Jack said as we made our way back toward the office to pick up his car.

"Jack, I'm rather tired," I protested. "I think I would like to take the day off and go home to flop on my bed."

"No cheesecake?" He looked so sweet, he was hard to resist.

"Well, maybe just one slice."

*The End*

# About the Author

**Laura S. Wharton** is the author of award-winning historical adventure novels suitable for young adult readers and adults. Her well-researched stories landed her on the Literary Trail of North Carolina, a coveted honor for a fiction writer. In addition to this novel, she is the author of *The Pirate's Bastard*, *Leaving Lukens*, *Deceived*, and *Stung!*, the riveting thriller/mysteries featuring Sam McClellan. She writes mysteries for children as well, often with children, to encourage a love of reading and writing.

Laura loves to tell a good story, and she revels in inspiring others to tell the stories around them. In fact, she encourages everyone she meets to use their imaginations as often as possible, and she has been known to tell classrooms of children to lie when they write to help them over the hurdles of knowing how to begin a story. (She hurriedly explains to shocked teachers and parents that being a novelist is probably the only profession where one can lie—and get away with it.) Her books are available wherever fine books are sold in paperback or in e-book formats, and she has other titles coming out soon for readers of all ages. Visit **www.LauraWhartonBooks.com** for more information on these and other new releases.

# Acknowledgments

I hope you have enjoyed reading this book as much as I've enjoyed researching and writing it. If you've read my other historical adventures, you know I am a bit of a research nerd. This story is no exception.

I extend a gracious thank you to the gentle people at the preservation organization, Historic Columbia, who work tirelessly to preserve the beautiful homes and gardens of Columbia, South Carolina. Without their thorough documentation of the garden restoration process of the Hampton-Preston Mansion in particular, my characters would have been less ambitious if left to my knowledge of garden restoration. The elegantly appointed Federal-style mansion was built in 1818 by Ainsley Hall, a merchant of Columbia. He and his wife, Sarah, sold the home to Wade Hampton I, in 1823, who updated the style to Greek revival. Under the ownership of the Hamptons and the direction of the mother and daughter team of Mary Cantey Hampton and Caroline Hampton Preston, the four acres of grounds were transformed into antebellum gardens containing native plants as well as eye-catching varieties from around the globe. In 2012, an ambitious revitalization began on the southern portion of the property. When I read through the immense amount of documentation on the restoration process, I knew that's where my story had to start. The Norton-Grace Mansion in this novel is based very loosely on the Hampton-Preston Mansion.

Speaking of preservation, my dear friend Claudia Deviney worked for years with North Carolina Preservation. Her passion for preservation—and the odd things found during such efforts—triggered an important plot point in this story. I give thanks for our longstanding friendship and the knowledge about this fascinating subject she's always willing to share. I hope I was able to channel some of her infectious passion for preservation in this story.

Chris Wishart is a real person who was the owner and chef extraordinaire with an incredibly real restaurant, Trio. His long-standing friendship with Lily McGuire is not real. In fact, they hadn't met until Chris read an advanced copy of the manuscript. It is with his blessing that I include him and his scrumptious cooking in this story. Chris' cooking is worth every precious calorie his patrons enjoy.

I would like to thank the following people who contributed their expertise and support: the kind folks at Broad Creek Press, my most excellent editor, Tyler Tichelaar, and interior designer, Shiloh Schroeder of Fusion

Creative Works, and Canadian artist Francois Thisdale for his sumptuous illustration on the cover.

Eric Latza is the inspiration for my Sensei in this story. As a karate instructor himself, he is extremely patient with his students young and old. He is also a sheriff's deputy, so I don't recommend messing with him outside his dojo.

The work of the artist mentioned in the Trade Street gallery showroom belongs to T. Bayley Wharton, my husband. I'm a fan of his work, of course, so I offer this gentle plug. His website is real as is his furniture, and he does regularly appear at the types of craft shows mentioned in this work. If you like the descriptions of his work in the story, you might like to search for his website online as a starting point (www.furniturexdesign.com).

To my author friends, Mary Flinn and Jane Tesh, who continue to encourage and support me, I say thank you for taking time from your busy writing schedules to help by listening to my ideas for this story and for early reviews of the manuscript. Your friendships mean so much to me. And a very special thank you goes to my longtime friend Kathy Field, whose knowledge of plants continues to amaze and astound me. It is Kathy who was able to sharpen my focus on certain plants and their toxicity levels that helped make this story realistic.

Finally, no project would be complete without saying a huge thank you to my parents, Don and Jane Spanton, who have always shared their love of the English language through words. Growing up in a house full of music, love, and laughter, I quickly learned the value of a good story, a snappy comment, and the proper timing needed for telling a well-crafted punch line of a joke. May the fun stories never end!

—Laura S. Wharton
2015

CPSIA information can be obtained
at www.ICGtesting.com
Printed in the USA
FFOW02n2022181115
18768FF